VIDEO MAGIC

(In Love at Northrupp High School)

Vikk Simmons

Printed in the United States of America

First Printing, 2005
Second Printing, 2015 (10th Anniversary Edition)

Cover Design by Thomas McGee, WriterlyDesigned.com
ISBN 978-1-941303-15-3

Ordinary Matters Publishing
PO Box 430577
Houston, Texas 777043
www.OrdinaryMattersPublishing.com

Praise for VIDEO MAGIC

"*Teenagers these days face more challenges than ever before. Vikk Simmons understands and confronts some of these important issues in VIDEO MAGIC.*" ~ Heather Ames, author

"*I loved this book from beginning to end. The main character was interesting and the plot kept me turning pages.*" — Read Too, Amazon reviewer

VIDEO MAGIC

WINNER OF THE
ROMANCE WRITERS OF AMERICA
GOLDEN HEART AWARD
FOR YOUNG ADULT NOVELS

Vikk Simmons

Praise for DIVIDED LOYALTIES

"Divided Loyalties is a cute story about the trials of high school. Full of angst, humor, and teenage crushes, this is a "G" rated book without any steamy scenes to offend younger readers. Vikk Simmons has an amazing ability to make the reader care for these characters. . . Overall, this is a wonderful afternoon read and is recommended for all readers of all ages." — Penny, Fallen Angels Review

"A great storyline with some deep emotional curves that truly make the reader think of where their own loyalties lay and why. A good read for the young adult that will make them stop and think of their own lives and the path they are taking." —Shirley Johnson, MidWest Book Review

"A wonderful story for any teen whose ever wondered whose side they're really on." — Kimberly Morris, author of 50 books for children and young adults, many of them for popular series including Mary-Kate and Ashley, Animorphs, Sweet Valley, and Generation Girl.

"Vikk Simmons is a wonderful storyteller. Her characters are engaging and believable. Divided Loyalties is a great book that deals with important issues in an entertaining and forthright manner while still being a great read." — Betty Traylor Gyenes, author of "Buckaroo" and "The Covering," ("The New Frontier: The Best of Today's Western Fiction"

"Young adult romances and fiction have come a long way, and DIVIDED LOYALTIES is a tale for today's teenaged girls that is sure to please. A great story with an underlying message for the modern world all in one package, it's difficult not to recommend this quick little ebook. Add DIVIDED LOYALTIES to your to-buy list soon and enjoy! — Amy Cunningham, Romance Reviews Today

Find out the latest romance news at Northrupp High and receive promotion information. :

NorthruppHighNews.com

How delicious is the winning
Of a kiss at Love's beginning

T. Campell
CLXXXIII Freedom and Love

Vikk Simmons

Table of Contents

FOREWARD

What would you do if one of your friends offered you an opportunity to work on a local movie production? Would you stop everything and go? That's what happened to me. One day I was working at my normal everyday job, hitting the computer keys all day long, and the next day I met up with my makeup artist friend and went with her to work on location for a local indie movie company as a production assistant during a 3-week long shoot. I had a wonderful time, despite the 20-hour work days, and my fictional story, VIDEO MAGIC, grew out of that experience.

Can't tell you how excited I am that this 10th anniversary edition of VIDEO MAGIC is being released on Valentine's Day weekend. I've always loved this story. You can't imagine how thrilled I was when VIDEO MAGIC won the Romance Writers of America national Golden Heart Award for Young Adults.

VIDEO MAGIC is the first book in my *In Love at Northrupp High* teen romance series. I'm so glad to have an opportunity to share this story and hope others will enjoy reading the sweet, romantic story of Kimberly and Greg. Love is not easy. Love is not always fair, but love is well-worth the effort.

Happy Reading!

Vikk Simmons
Houston, February 14, 2015

Vikk Simmons

CHAPTER ONE

K imberly Lange stood by the long row of classroom windows, closed her eyes and wished really, really hard. Please, please let it be me. Everybody loves a winner.

The video club meeting was about to begin, and in a matter of minutes Kimberly's fate would be decided. The thing she wanted most in the world was to be the intern on the senior video project at Houston's Northrupp High School. Kimberly pictured Mr. Jeffries, tall and thin, standing in front of the room ready to call out the name of the one junior who would be chosen to work on the project. "Me, me, me," she whispered, allowing her imagination to carry her forward in time. "And the winner is...Kimberly Lange."

"You wish." Behind her, an irritating but familiar voice broke into her fantasy. "Jeffries isn't about to pick you. After all, Greg asked me to run for the spot. He is the head of the project this year."

Embarrassed at being overheard, Kimberly turned to find Marla Morgan, the reigning drama diva, standing barely three feet away. Marla was one of those girls you love to hate. With long, silky copper-red hair that hung down her back and barely brushed her tiny waist, she grabbed the attention of everyone in the room when she made an entrance. Of course, the short leopard print skirt, chocolate brown lacey wrap top and kick-ass wedgies didn't hurt. She had that runway model look. Not surprising since she'd been doing the local model thing since middle grade.

"No one was talking to you," Kimberly defended herself, and stood her ground as Marla gave her the once over, a long, exaggerated look that took in all of Kimberly's tall form from head to toe. "I've got as good a chance as you to win."

Marla growled—that's what it sounded like to Kimberly—and turned away, dismissing Kimberly and stalking to the front of the class where she dropped her pink and black bag on the floor and curled her body into a chair, front row center. Kimberly stared at her. She watched Marla pull out her phone and begin text messaging someone. She knew Marla had the inside track to the internship. Everyone knew she and Greg Winters were big time pals. Marla had somehow made her way into the group that surrounded Greg and helped him with his video projects the last couple of years. She had even "starred" in several. Because Greg had been chosen as the one junior to work on the senior video project last year as the intern, he would be in charge of this year's production. If the pick depended upon Greg only, Kimberly was sure the choice would fall to Marla.

The door opened again to allow in the only one at Northrupp who could surpass Marla in the drama diva department. Carol Nelson, the reigning Goth Queen of Northrupp, entered wearing her Goth proudly. Deep purple slashed across the top of her raven black hair and accentuated the short style that framed her face. Wayward wisps highlighted her pale skin, black eyebrows and black pouty lips. Dressed all in black, Carol garnered plenty of attention everywhere she went. Next to her, Kimberly was a ghost—and way too normal looking. Ricardo also came into the room, following in Carol's wake, but instead of joining Carol and Kimberly, he wandered over to Marla.

Kimberly could tell by the look on Carol's face that she was not pleased.

"I don't know why Ricardo has to talk to that girl when he knows I hate it," Carol said, joining Kimberly at the long row of windows.

Kimberly knew Ricardo worshiped the ground Carol walked on but that never seemed to get through her best friend's thick skull. The two had a constant battle because of Carol's insecurities. Sure, Ricardo was one cute guy but Kimberly knew Carol didn't need to worry. Ricardo bent over Marla, probably to look at the messages on her phone, and Kimberly heard Carol take in a quick breath that sounded more like a hiss. What was up with all the cat metaphors today, she wondered and made a mental promise to stop.

"You've got nothing to worry about, girl," she said and turned back to the window. "He's not interested in her."

Carol chose to ignore Kimberly's reassurance and said, instead, "You're here early. Waiting to give Mr. J one last pitch?"

"Mr. Jeffries isn't here yet, can't you tell?" Marla called out, not bothering to look at either one of them, preferring, instead, to keep a tight focus on Ricardo. "I'm sure he's seen and heard enough of your friend."

"And you," Carol answered and leaned closer to Kimberly. "Why they let Miss It's-All-About-Me in to this thing is beyond me."

"I heard that."

"Oh, I forgot, her highness is blessed with bat ears."

"Will you stop?" Kimberly said before Marla could respond. "Give it a rest, both of you."

Marla turned back to Ricardo and kept him talking, but the constant tap of her pencil on the table top was a clear giveaway that she, too, was nervous. Maybe Marla's not so sure of herself, Kimberly thought.

Carol leaned in and whispered into Kimberly's ear. "Maybe it's not Mr. J but Greg you were hoping to catch early."

"Stop," Kimberly said and pulled away from Carol. She felt the quick hot flash that warmed her neck and tried to check the blush blooming on her cheeks. "I just want to get this over, all right?"

The rest of the video club streamed into the classroom and let their backpacks drop to the floor or pile on the tables as they pulled out chairs and sat down. Some flipped open their cell phones to make calls or text message friends. A few mumbled a hello here and there.

Carol gave a quick exasperated sigh and signaled for Ricardo to join them, and the three slid into chairs at the back of the room.

"Don't worry, chica," Ricardo said to Kimberly. "You're gonna beat Cat Woman over there."

Kimberly groaned inwardly and smiled. "Thanks."

"No, I mean it."

"You know something? Did Marla say anything?" Carol whispered. "What is it? Tell me."

Ricardo shrugged. Before he could answer Greg Winters entered the room. Tall and broad-shouldered, with unruly, curly brown hair that refused to be tamed, Greg had a boyish charm that made the girls of Northrupp High melt. Dressed in worn jeans, a t-shirt, and wearing his Northrupp High baseball team cap facing backward, Greg walked to the front of the room. He carried a large folder full of pages, probably the script for his film, and pulled out several sheets of paper.

His quiet presence commanded even more attention than Marla's. She slipped out of her chair and joined him. Greg smiled when he saw her. Friends for years, they had history. Kimberly wasn't exactly sure what kind of history, but Carol swore the two had been boyfriend-girlfriend at one time. Whatever. Greg had made it clear he wanted Jeffries to choose Marla.

Marla rushed forward to pick up a couple of the papers and taped them to the blackboard, all the while talking to Greg. Kimberly wished she could hear their conversation. Even more, she wished for a little history of her own with Greg. He had to be one of the most popular seniors, but he didn't date much. She'd seen him around, and they'd bumped into each other during the video club meetings, but they'd never said much more than a hello to one another. Strange, since he was Ricardo's best friend. Carol had been trying to fix the two of them up for months, but their schedules never meshed. Ricardo said Greg had way too many family responsibilities, and he seldom had time to date.

"Hey, everyone, listen up," Greg said.

Chairs scraped as the kids turned to face the front, push aside their backpacks, and flipped shut their cell phones. He had their attention.

"I'll just go over a few things while we wait for Mr. Jeffries."

One of the kids called out, "Hey, you gonna tell us who got the intern job?"

"Are you?" Marla asked. "I know you know."

Greg shook his curly head, and Kimberly had a sudden desire to run her fingers through his hair. She imagined his hair was soft and easy to twirl. "Nope," he said. "Not a chance and I don't know." Pointing to the pages on the blackboard, he continued, "Here's the storyboard for the video. I've been working on it for months, and I think we're going to have a good entry."

"Yeah, we know. You and Marla have been working real hard," said one of the boys sitting next to Marla.

Greg flashed a rare kilowatt smile and shook his head. "Marla hasn't even seen this yet."

"True, so true," Marla said. "I tried but he wouldn't let me. He's like a big old mama bear with his storyboard. Won't let any of his baby bears touch it."

"Oh barf," Carol said and rolled her eyes.

Everyone in the room chuckled. Everyone knew about Greg's storyboard obsession. While most filmmakers keep their options open and their storyboards loose, Greg was the opposite. No one could touch it once he had it blocked out.

And everyone knew how he felt about making changes late in the filming. At least he knew what he was doing. Last year's senior video made the top three in the annual district competition. He had been the intern and had played a big part in its development. Kimberly could only guess at how much pressure he had to be feeling this year now that he was the head of the senior project. Everyone expected Greg would take them to the number one spot this year. She certainly did. That's why she wanted the internship so much. An award-winning video would be a big plus on her resume. Of course, getting to know Greg Winters better had to be another big plus.

"Okay, so you all know how I feel about these pages," he said, smiling. "Don't touch them. Stay on the schedule. Got it?"

Everyone yelled back, "Got it."

Mr. Jeffries, teacher and sponsor of the video club, walked to the front of the class. With each step, Kimberly's anxiety level increased. It would only be a matter of minutes now.

He took a moment and looked out over the room full of students, then grinned. "Guess we better get this over, right?"

Kimberly had to agree.

He opened a folded piece of paper and began calling out names and their positions on the film. "Greg, director/writer/camera, of course; Barry, producer; Ricardo, camera; Carol, make-up and casting; Nelson, audio; Sam, lights.... " No surprises there, Kimberly thought.

He continued to call out names until only two remained: Marla and Kimberly.

Vikk Simmons

CHAPTER TWO

Major butterflies flitted about in Kimberly's stomach. It was now or never. She couldn't tell from Mr. Jeffries's face whether she or Marla had won the intern position, but it was clear what Marla thought. She had a big, disgusting, happy grin on her face as she smoothed her long copper-red hair and played with the ends.

Carol leaned over and squeezed Kimberly's hand. "Don't worry, it'll be you."

Kimberly nodded, but she didn't have as much confidence as Carol.

"Really," Carol whispered. "You can't miss with that video you submitted. You did way more than you had to. I doubt Marla did anything."

"She didn't have to," Kimberly replied. "She had Greg."

Ricardo leaned in front of Carol to talk to Kimberly. "Don't worry. Jeffries is a fair man, you'll see."

Kimberly hoped he was right.

Mr. Jeffries held a sheet of paper up and began. "This year we had two great candidates apply for the internship; both came with impressive experience and both would do the job equally well; but there can be only one." He glanced around the room then settled his gaze on Kimberly, who suddenly realized she'd become the center of attention. "This year's winner went the extra mile and spent the summer months shooting a video to include in her submission—a very good video."

She'd done it. Butterflies took flight and were replaced by a new inner calm. Kimberly knew Mr. Jeffries had chosen her even before he said her name.

"Kimberly Lange is our intern for this year's project," Mr. Jeffries announced and began clapping. "Congratulations."

The rest of the students joined in the clapping while Carol jumped up, nearly knocking her chair over, to give Kimberly a big hug, saying, "I knew it. I knew it. I knew it."

Ricardo smiled and walked around to give her a hug. "Told you," he whispered.

Kimberly was at a loss for words. In a matter of seconds, the video club swarmed around her. Not only would she be this year's intern, but she'd head next year's project. In the midst of the congratulations, Kimberly saw Marla standing off to the side talking to Greg. Her hands were in motion as she spoke, and Greg leaned in, listening intently. She couldn't help but notice how good the two of them looked together. Would they come over and join everyone else? Kimberly wasn't sure.

"Marla," Mr. Jeffries called. He towered over the group of students crowding Kimberly.

Marla broke off her conversation and looked up. Jeffries waved them over to everyone else. Greg had his arm around Marla's shoulders, and Kimberly couldn't help but wonder again if they were dating. Marla couldn't be that upset. She'd made it plain that she was only running for the internship because Greg had asked her to. Marla had one big desire: to be a famous actress. Nothing else seemed to matter to her. Everyone knew she joined the club so she could star in the video club's films and documentaries. She had become part of Greg's inner circle. Kimberly knew who made up the in-crowd because they all hung out together in the cafeteria during lunch and after school. Ricardo had invited her to join them several times,but Kimberly had declined because of Carol's intense dislike of Marla. She couldn't leave her best friend just to be part of the Greg Winters crowd.

"Good job," Marla said, the big smile still plastering her face.

By now the smile had to be fake. Probably just another acting job for the glorious diva. Still, Kimberly smiled back hoping the tension between them would drop a level or two now that their competition was over.

"Marla's been taking care of the camera equipment, but as of today, you'll take on that duty," Mr. Jeffries said. "Greg will fill you in on what jobs he'll need you to do."

For the first time that day, Greg smiled at Kimberly. She noticed how the corners of his eyes crinkled into a sudden burst of lines like the sun's rays. "Glad you'll be working with us, Kimberly."

She liked the way he said her name. His soft Texas drawl made it inviting. She watched as his eyes picked up the filtered afternoon light streaming through the blinds. They reminded her of clear, running mountain water, and a warm feeling washed over her as she returned his smile. "Thanks. I can't wait to begin."

"I know Marla will show you around the equipment," he said, seeming to respond to her enthusiasm. "Thanks to some generous alumni, we have a new digital camera, which is truly awesome and will give us a terrific film-like image."

"Yeah, wait till you see. You'll love it," Ricardo said, his black eyes gleaming at the thought.

"Cool," Kimberly answered. "That should put us way out in front of the competition."

"Definitely," Mr. Jeffries added. "Why don't you and Marla plan to meet after school tomorrow so she can show you all the equipment. We start shooting Saturday." Turning to Marla, he finished, "Don't forget to show her the new lenses."

Before she could ask anything, Greg spoke. "You'll be working a lot with the camera crew—that's me, Ricardo, Sam, and Nelson—so you need to stay on top of the storyboard and make sure the equipment is ready to go." He turned to include Marla. "Anything you need to know, just check with me or Marla. We've worked with the equipment for the last month or two and are pretty familiar with it by now."

Greg's voice filled with passion, and she noted how his speech revved up whenever he talked about the camera or some other aspect of the video. She understood. She had the same reaction. Marla, on the other hand, did not. All she cared about was being center stage and emoting all over the place.

"Listen up, everyone," Greg said, his voice getting slightly louder to be heard over the various conversations as the students went back to their chairs to gather their stuff. "We'll be shooting in the Henderson Building Saturday morning. Be there at eight, sharp."

A couple of the kids groaned, but Kimberly knew it was all in fun.

Then Greg turned back to Kimberly, Ricardo, Marla and a few others. "The rest of you meet me here in the parking lot at five a.m. We'll load up the equipment and head on out to the building to set up."

"Omygod, you surely don't expect me to be here at that hour, do you?" Carol asked, her eyes saucer-like.

Ricardo grinned at Carol's horrified reaction. Carol had the internal clock of a vampire preferring the night to day and preferring to skip mornings altogether whenever she could. Kimberly wasn't a true morning person, either, but for her it was less of a struggle to get up early. She figured Carol would be setting multiple alarm clocks to be sure she made the early call.

Greg rolled his eyes. "You'll need to be at the building and set up for make-up before the eight o'clock call, okay?"

"Sure," Carol said and made a quick cross over her heart.

Greg and Marla pulled down the storyboard and gathered up their things while Kimberly digested the fact that she was now the official intern. In the corner, Carol and Ricardo said their good-byes.

Thirty minutes later Carol dropped Kimberly off at her house and drove off. Kimberly couldn't wait to tell her parents the news. She'd practiced how she'd tell them all the way home with Carol first playing the role of her mother, then her father. She pushed open the side door, dropped her backpack on the washing room folding table and burst into the kitchen.

"Mom, Mom," she called but her mother wasn't in the kitchen. She gave a second yell. "Hey Mom, anyone here? I've got BIG news."

Kimberly opened the refrigerator door and pulled out a diet cola, then grabbed a warm chocolate chip cookie from a plate piled high on the kitchen counter. "Mom," she yelled. "I'm home."

"What is it?" her mother called as she came into the kitchen. "You'd think there was a fire in here."

"Umm, Mom," Kimberly mumbled in between cookie bites. "You won't believe what happened today—"

"I'm so glad you're home—"

"Mom, I'm trying to tell you something."

"I hear you, honey, but I have a surprise, too."

Kimberly stopped eating the cookie. "I got it. I got the job."

"What? Oh, that's nice, honey. We knew you could do it," her mother said, "but come to the living room. Guess who's come home for a visit? Talk about good news."

Kimberly groaned, and her stomach flipped. Only one person could account for her mother's lack of reaction. She tossed the rest of the cookie into the garbage and tried to hide her disappointment.

"Hey there, Kimbo, ready for a bear hug?"

CHAPTER THREE

Bobby.

Kimberly didn't know whether she should be glad or mad to see her older brother. As tall as she was, her big brother was the Jolly Green Giant. He had to duck whenever he walked into the kitchen so he wouldn't bump his head. When they were growing up, her father had to take up the chain to the dining room chandelier because Bobby kept bumping into it whenever he leaned across the dining room table. Kimberly considered their tall gene a curse. Bobby seemed to revel in his size. She and Bobby were seven years apart, and he'd been living in Austin ever since he graduated from high school. They rarely saw him except for holidays, so she had no idea why he had driven all the way to Houston in the middle of the week. She had a pretty good idea that it wasn't to say hello to his kid sister.

"Hey, Sis, what's up?"

"What are you doing here?"

"Kimberly, that's no way to say hello to your brother," her mother said. "He's got some great news to share, don't you hon?"

Kimberly's heart sank. She loved her brother, but why did he have to upstage her every time? "Figures. So what's your great news?" she asked, not really wanting an answer. Wasn't it just like Bobby to mess up her plans?

"Oh, shouldn't we wait until your father gets home?" her mother said, giving her brother a little pat on the chest.

Kimberly couldn't believe it. Her mother had apparently already forgotten about her good news about the internship but couldn't stop talking about Bobby's. No way did she want to wait until her father got home. She wanted him to spill it now.

"Oh, just tell me," she said, not even trying to keep the bitterness out of her voice. She stared at her preppy brother and waited.

Bobby laughed, his voice deep and rich, which only served to irritate Kimberly even more. "You won't believe it, Kimbo, but I got a phone call the other day telling me I've been awarded a Macarthur Fellowship."

"What's that?"

"Oh, just a little award that comes with a big check: $50,000.00."

"Isn't that wonderful, honey?" her mother said, gushing. She patted his chest again. "Your father and I are so proud of you."

Oh, that's wonderful, all right, Kimberly thought. As if skipping grades at Northrupp and attending college two years early wasn't bad enough for her to deal with — plus that little matter of being a U.S. Senate Page one summer — now he'd won a major prize that overshadowed anything Kimberly could ever do. Kimberly felt her confidence seeping away.

"Terrific, Bobby. That's great." Her words sounded hollow, but she didn't care. She was tired of always coming in second. Why bother? Her own mother didn't think her getting the internship was any big deal, so why should she? She didn't need to share her news with her brother or with anyone else, for that matter.

"Do you know your brother is the youngest ever to receive a Macarthur Fellowship?" her mother asked, seemingly oblivious to Kimberly's reaction to her brother's news. "I looked it up on the computer—"

"Don't tell me, you Googled it?" Kimberly said, trying not to groan. Ever since she'd shown her mother how to do searches on the Internet, her mother had gone Google-happy. She looked up everything: recipes, family history, book reviews, you name it.

"Yes, I looked it up," her mother said. "What's wrong with that? I wanted to know all about this Macarthur thing."

Yeah, so you can share it with the whole world, Kimberly thought. "I'm going upstairs."

"That's all you're going to say?" Her mother asked, her disappointment clearly showing. "That was hardly a rousing 'congratulations' earlier. I would think you'd be happy for him."

"I am happy, Mom," she said and barely gave her brother a glance. "Congratulations, Bobby."

With that, Kimberly left the kitchen and took the stairs two by two. She slammed her bedroom door shut when she was safely inside her sanctuary. She had to get as far away as possible from her boy-wonder brother who could do no wrong and from her mother who only seemed to have eyes for Bobby.

It just wasn't fair, she thought. Even now, after Bobby had been out of the house for so many years, she still fell under his large and looming shadow. Would it ever lift?

She remembered how happy she was when Jeffries called out her name. She believed she'd never come down off of that high, but she had been dead wrong. Just once, she thought, couldn't her mom be happy for her—just her? Kimberly's disappointment increased with each thought. All her life it had been Bobby, Bobby, and Bobby. Why couldn't her parents see her and her accomplishments? Why couldn't they love her the way they loved her brother?

Tears slipped out of her eyes and slid down her cheeks despite her best efforts to keep them from falling. The comfort of her room with its competing purple, lavender and lime green striped walls barely lifted her mood. She tossed her shoes off, kicking them high in the air only to land on the hot pink bean bag chair Carol had given her as a birthday present the year before. Her fingers found the CD player. Maybe she could drown out her self-pity with music.

After a few minutes, she looked over at the computer. Surely Carol would be online by now. Kimberly got up and logged in to her email account.

She stared at her empty buddy list. Where was everyone?

Disgusted, she threw herself onto her bed, piled high with pillows and stuffed animals. She nestled deep into them and tried to forget all about her mother and her brother. She replayed Jeffries calling out her name. If only she could hold onto that sweet memory forever. She'd worked so hard for it. For two years, she'd planned and prepared to apply for the internship. Now she had won. Not only that, she had the great luck to work with someone like Greg.

Thoughts of Greg tumbled through her mind, and she remembered the light in his eyes and the warmth of his voice. Cute didn't even come close. She'd had her eye on him ever since she first saw him. She remembered how excited he was when the club's documentary placed in the last year's contest. She'd almost swear his hair curled tighter and grew more out of control. Everyone said the video couldn't have made it without his help. Even the seniors said so. No wonder everyone had such great expectations this year with him as project leader. Now, with the new camera, how could they do anything but come in first?

She couldn't wait for Saturday. Surely, her video would help them see her as the huge asset she knew she could be. She'd spent most of her summer vacation making the video. She'd gotten the idea from a website that encouraged teens to take action. Every year they held a contest with a $500 award going to the best community service project done by a teen or a group of teens. Kimberly knew of a teen who'd started a simple food drive for the hungry last year that turned into a major deal between two rivalry schools. Using the annual football game as the centerpiece, she'd urged everyone in her school to bring canned goods for the food drive to the stadium that night. When the other school heard about it, they decided to match them. The food drive raised so much attention that the local media came out and covered the event. Kimberly knew the event was a good idea for a video, so she contacted the teen. A couple of months later, she had her submission for the contest. It would be months they would announce the winners.

When it came time to put in her application for the internship, Kimberly had almost left the video out. It had been an afterthought, really. Now she was glad she'd followed through.

If she hadn't, Jeffries might have given the internship to Marla instead.

But he didn't. Saturday she'd be working side by side with Greg—a thought that made her really happy. She hoped Greg would take advantage of her skills and let her help Ricardo with the camera. For sure, she didn't want to wind up being some little gopher, going here and there, doing odds and ends for everyone. She had a lot more to give to the project than that. If Greg didn't see it right away, she'd just have to show him.

Visions of working with Greg flashed through her mind. Then she thought about Marla. Kimberly wondered again if Marla was upset. Why would she be? She had no interest in the technical stuff. If it weren't for Greg, Kimberly knew Marla would have never applied for the position. She hoped Greg's obvious preference of Marla over her wouldn't get in the way of their working together.

Together. There's that word again, she thought. She had to admit Greg was a true hottie. Was she foolish to think he and Marla were just pals? Carol seemed to think so. Of course, Carol was always pairing up people. She even suspected Marla of going after Ricardo—and that was really stupid. Ricardo insisted Greg and Marla were just friends. He should know. If so, Kimberly realized, it was a close friendship.

What was it like to be close to Greg? Hot, she thought. Real hot. If his smile made her warm, what would his touch do? After a mere nanosecond of that thought, Kimberly knew she had to shift gears. That was a little too hot.

But she couldn't deny Greg's passion and intensity. What would it be like working with him? He cared about making films. She understood that; she lived for the camera. Nothing calmed her down more than to be behind the lens. One day she'd be a cinematographer; she'd go to Hollywood. She knew she had the talent—just like Greg.

Kimberly stared up at the photographs that lined her bedroom's four walls. She had done them all, and each one carried a memory of days past. Days when she and Carol had gone to the park and visited the zoo; days when she had done weekly walkabouts to capture the varied face of Houston's cityscape; more days when friends posed for more and more photos. All to help Kimberly develop her photography skills. Her absolute favorite image had to be the one that showed Carol being Extreme Goth Woman poised over a water fountain at the zoo. A giraffe had leaned over the fence and managed to get low enough to get his face in the photo. Talk about a strange contrast. Kimberly loved it.

About contrast, she thought. What about the differences between her and Marla? Kimberly hoped Marla wouldn't become a drama queen tomorrow when she handed over the equipment. The last thing Kimberly wanted was some big scene with Marla displaying major attitude.

She shook her head as if by doing so she could prevent it from happening. No more Marla. Kimberly needed to keep her focus zoomed in on the important things like the internship and all she'd be able to do during this project.

She couldn't wait.

CHAPTER FOUR

Marla was late.

Kimberly paced up and down the visual arts classroom where the video club held their meeting yesterday. Surely Marla hadn't forgotten she was to turn over the camera equipment and demonstrate the new camera to Kimberly. She stared out the window for a few minutes then returned to her marathon walk up and down the room.

Suddenly the door opened and in walked the missing diva. True to form, she didn't say a word, just went to the large storage cabinet at the back of the room. Even without the leopard skirt, the girl slinked. Marla pulled out a key and opened the doors. Inside, Kimberly saw one of the camera bags. Marla brought it out and unzipped the bag to reveal the contents.

"This is the new camera everyone was talking about yesterday," she said in a monotone. "Over here are the new lenses. Be careful with all of it. It cost a fortune, and we're lucky to have them."

Kimberly didn't say anything, although she certainly felt like it. Marla's preachy tone didn't invite friendly conversation. "Can you show me how it all goes together?"

Marla took the camera out of the bag and gave a brief demonstration. Then she showed Kimberly where the lights were kept, the scrims stored, and the boom mike held. The entire process took barely fifteen minutes, and Marla didn't leave any room for questions.

Kimberly figured she was still mad from coming in second place the day before.

Marla turned away to put everything back in its rightful place before she faced Kimberly. "You need to keep track of the batteries and be sure they're fully charged. You don't want to run out. I make it a practice to charge them after each use so they're ready to go."

"Thanks, I'll remember that," Kimberly said, trying to ignore Marla's mood. Like Kimberly didn't know to recharge a battery. However, Marla did have a point. Kimberly decided to follow the same practice of recharging the batteries before putting them away.

"Greg is great at what he does. Don't screw it up. We have a real chance of winning this year."

"I don't know what you think I could do but you can bet I'm not going to screw things up." Kimberly took the two batteries Marla handed her and slipped them into the blue carrying case.

"Greg told me to tell you he and Ricardo will pick up the equipment at five a.m. Saturday morning, but you can go directly to the Henderson Building. Just be there by seven a.m.. The security guard will let you in. Just tell him who you are and that you're with the film crew."

"I can be here early Saturday morning. It's not a problem."

Marla shrugged. "Your call. But it's not necessary. I wouldn't show up until I had to. That's why I won't be there until much later in the morning."

"You're going to be there?" Kimberly asked.

"Oh, Carol didn't tell you? She cast me in the lead." Marla barely hid the smile that played at the corner of her pouty blood red lips. "She had to, you know. Greg always wants me in his productions."

Kimberly suppressed a groan. She should have known she couldn't leave Marla behind that easily. She was a natural to play the lead, a better actress than she'd have been an intern.

"Great," Kimberly answered. She put the camera bag back on the shelf and closed the cabinet's double doors. Without asking, she took the key out of Marla's hand and locked the doors. "I guess I'll see you there."

Then she put the key on her key ring and left Marla standing in the classroom, alone.

* * *

Saturday morning arrived, and Carol picked Kimberly up for the morning shoot. She had already stopped at the convenience store and picked up her jumbo cup of hot coffee and a large blueberry muffin. A cranberry muffin for Kimberly was in the bag on the seat. Carol had piled the back of her car high with zebra-striped sheets, a short bar stool, and a make-shift frame to create her "make-up cage." The Cage, the name Carol used for her portable make-up room, would be the arena where she worked her magic on the actor's faces.

Even in October Houston could be hot, so Kimberly had dressed in jean shorts and a simple v-necked top. Carol never thought Kimberly used enough make-up. Light on the lipstick, she had opted for a raspberry gloss. She did think about wearing the never-worn wedgies with three-inch heels that she had stashed in her closet but decided, once again, against them. She was too tall. Wearing those shoes would turn her into an Amazon. She didn't want to tower over anyone, especially Greg. Instead, she had opted for the slip-on tennis shoes.

Carol was her usual shimmering self in basic black dress and in a mood. After riding back and forth to school with her the last two months, Kimberly knew Carol wouldn't get any better until she'd consumed a tank full of coffee.

"Thanks for picking me up," Kimberly said as she opened the bag and pulled out her muffin. "My mom's promised to take me to get my driver's test next week. Then I won't have to bum rides from you all the time."

"No problem," Carol said, picking up the cup of coffee.

When they arrived at the parking garage, Carol dropped Kimberly off at the elevator and charged her with the care of her make-up case. She'd meet Kimberly in the lobby after she parked the car.

The elevator door whooshed open, and Kimberly found herself in the way. Someone was trying to lug several bright orange bags and an awkward rectangular shield while backing out of the elevator. In the process, he knocked Kimberly down.

"Watch out," she yelled, as she put her hands out to break her fall. The make-up case slipped out of her grasp and hit the ground. The latch broke, spilling its contents everywhere.

The shield, what Kimberly recognized as a scrim or light shield, had caught on the elevator door and whoever was behind it had clearly not realized he'd knocked her down.

"Sorry. The building's closed. Only Northrupp High's video club is allowed in," he said. Then he gave the shield one last tug and stumbled backward. When it came loose, he tripped over the case and fell on top of her.

"Get off me," she cried and pushed and shoved to get him off. "Look at this mess."

Kimberly crawled on her hands and knees as she tried to pick up the jars, lipsticks and nail polish that had scattered around her and throw them into the case. Carol would probably be mad when she saw the mess. It wasn't until she grabbed the outstretched hand that she looked up.

Greg Winters tightened his grip and pulled her up. "Sorry."

She cursed her luck. How embarrassing. She looked down at her knees. At least she hadn't scratched herself up in the fall. She scrambled to stand up. "You know, you almost tore the scrim," she said, pointing to the light diffuser shield. "And I am with the club."

"Hey, I'm really sorry about all this," he said. "I didn't mean to run into you. Are you all right?"

She stooped down and threw the last few lipsticks and jars into the make-up case and snapped it shut. "I'm fine."

Kimberly was more embarrassed than hurt. She hated knowing he'd witnessed her sprawled out on the concrete floor with all her stuff strewn about — although it was his fault.

"Can I help you—"

"No, no, I'm fine."

"I didn't mean to be so curt...in the beginning, I mean. I couldn't' see you." Greg picked up the bags and the scrim. "I guess it's not much of an excuse."

"No problem. Uhmm, I'm just on my way up...."

"Yeah," he said and picked up the bags. "We won't need as much equipment as I expected, so I thought I'd get some of it out of the way." He carried them over to the van parked next to the elevator and tossed them into the back. Then he eased the scrim into a flat cardboard box and wedged it against several carriers for portable light fixtures. "You'll find everyone in the lobby."

Kimberly nodded and hit the button again. This time the elevator doors opened to an empty elevator. She stepped inside and punched the "L" button. The elevator's doors closed, leaving her with an image of Greg leaning against the van and rolling a sweating iced water bottle against his forehead. Headaches already?

When the doors opened, she walked into chaos. Voices boomed back and forth, shouting directions. Students carried equipment and scurried across the lobby. She felt an adrenalin rush as she stepped out of the elevator and into the frenzied activity. This was what she lived for.

A few minutes later, Carol entered the main lobby pulling a cart piled high with the rest of her tricks of the trade. She quickly set up the "cage" and filled a table with fishing tackle boxes and cans of all sizes. She opened the make-up case and looked at Kimberly.

"Sorry, I had a bit of an accident. Greg bumped into me and knocked me down. The case fell open, and everything went everywhere."

Carol tried not to laugh. "Are you all right?"

"Yes, not even scratched. But it was embarrassing."

"I bet," Carol said as she sorted through the makeup brushes, hair spray, and bottles and jars. She still looked as though she was trying not to smile when she said, "You better go find Greg and get the equipment squared away. Ricardo is already up there."

"Where's there?"

"Third floor."

Kimberly turned and started for the elevator.

"Hey," Carol called out. "Send Marla over if you see her. She's late for make- up."

Kimberly would, but she remembered Marla had said she'd be in much later. Evidently she didn't get the word about the early makeup call. Then again, thinking about Marla, maybe she decided to ignore the early call. When Kimberly stepped off the elevator on the third floor, she saw Greg right away. She tried to ignore the soft flap of a butterfly deep within her as she walked toward him. He still had the Northrupp cap on, and his hands were jammed deep into the back pockets of his jeans. He was talking to Ricardo and someone else she didn't recognize.

"Greg, come over here, man. We've got a few problems."

Kimberly stayed off on the sidelines and watched Greg as he took the camera. He had an almost reverent way of handling the camera, a real soft touch she understood all too well.

"Carol, anyone seen Carol?" a high-pitched voice cried.

Kimberly stared at the red-headed boy dressed in red and white sweats with a whistle on a rope, hanging around his neck. When he reached her, he wrapped his arms around her like she was some long lost friend." Tell me, you haven't seen Carol, have you?"

Kimberly tried not to grin. "Yeah, I came here with her. She's downstairs."

"Thank you, hon. You're a wonder," he said. "Now, who are you? One of the actors?"

This time Kimberly laughed. "No, no, I'm the intern."

"Oh-h-h-h, the intern. I remember now. It's Kimberly, right?" Barry stepped back and looked her up and down. "Say, do you know anything about following a script? I need someone to check continuity today."

"I'm sure Greg wants me to stay with the equipment—"

"Don't worry about him, hon. I can take care of the big bad wolf over there. Just tell me if you want to do it."

"Sure."

Kimberly's bravado vanished as soon as Barry walked off. She knew the importance of continuity. The job came with an enormous amount of responsibility. Still, so did the cameras and lenses and all the other equipment. She was up to the task.

"So, Barry tells me you're going to take over continuity?"

Kimberly turned to find Greg. "Just for today, I hope you don't mind."

"It would have been nice if you checked with me first," he said, not trying to cover up his irritation. "You'll have to find a way to work it out somehow. I need you to help Ricardo and Nelson set up."

A thrill ran through her when she realized she'd be handling the equipment. "I can do both," she said quickly and left to find Ricardo.

He had plenty for her to do. She helped unpack the light equipment, checked stands, bulbs, cords and extensions. Before she knew it, an hour had passed, and she hadn't even noticed Marla had arrived. She stood off to the side, practicing her lines.

She had forgotten all about Marla. She went over to tell her Carol was waiting for her when she suddenly heard Greg. His voice was sharp and angry. "Where's Kimberly? We've got a real problem."

CHAPTER FIVE

K imberly turned to see Greg, obviously upset, cradling the camera with the battery flap open and one of the batteries in the palm of his hand. He lifted his hand and spoke to her. "Didn't you check the camera out yesterday when you and Marla were going over the equipment?"

She had no idea what he was talking about. "Check it out?"

"Yes, check it out," he repeated. "Didn't you check the batteries? Neither one has been recharged. How are we going to get all our shooting done today on time if the blasted batteries aren't fully charged?"

She could tell by the rapid fire of his words and the dark scowl on his face that she had made a major error in judgment. She stared at the batteries, and then slipped a look past him to Marla and wondered why she hadn't followed her own practice of recharging the batteries after each use?

"I—"

"Never mind, I don't need excuses. What I need are fully charged batteries. Take the extra one and get the recharging started. We'll just have to do as much as we can with this one battery and hope the other will be fully-charged by the time we're ready. As it is, it looks as though we're going to lose an hour or more."

"I should be able to get them fully charged—"

"We have to be out of here by noon. No matter what you do, we're going to have lost time today."

Kimberly took the battery out of Greg's outstretched hand, and then reached for the second one in the side pocket of the camera bag. Why had she trusted Marla? Kimberly knew Greg had a right to be angry with her. She got the second battery recharging, then checked the charge on the first one. She hoped the second one would be fully-charged by the time the first one ran out of juice. She slipped the battery into the camera and looked for Greg. She saw him over by the stairwell where he was blocking out new directions for Ricardo and Marla.

"No problemo, Kimmy," Barry said, appearing out of nowhere and throwing his arm around her shoulders. "Greg's a genius when it comes to this stuff. He'll be able to shoot around the problem."

"Kimberly, my name is Kimberly," she said. She knew he was only trying to help, but she didn't feel all that comforted. She'd made a major screw up—and on her first day as an intern.

"Kimberly, then," Barry said, giving her shoulder a squeeze. "Don't look so down in the dumps. It's not the end of the world."

She stared at him.

"Okay, maybe it's not the best thing that could have happened but it's also not the worst. Try to keep your perspective."

"Sure, Barry, I'll try," she said.

"What's up girlfriend?" Carol asked, suddenly appearing out of nowhere. "I heard you're right in the middle of a problem."

Barry gave Kimberly one last squeeze and said, "Time's wasting. I'll leave you here with your gal pal." Then he sped off in the direction of Ricardo and Greg.

Kimberly bent down to pick up the script for the next scene Greg would be shooting. Marla would be center stage, of course.

"Earth to Kimberly," Carol prompted. "What's up? You look lost," Carol said, waving her hand in front of Kimberly's face.

Kimberly returned to the present and to Carol's presence. "Nothing, I guess. I was thinking about Marla—"

"Don't worry about it. She showed up for make-up."

"No, I—"

"What about her? Did she say or do something?"

"No, I mean, I don't think she would do anything...."

Carol spun around and looked for Marla. She would have marched over to the girl if Kimberly hadn't put her hand out to hold her back. "I don't know for sure if she did anything on purpose."

"Then what?" Carol stared at Marla for a few more seconds then turned her attention back to Kimberly. "What happened?"

"I just made a big mistake. I don't know how I could have been so careless," Kimberly said, although she knew full well why she didn't check the batteries. "I assumed the batteries had already been recharged and didn't check them yesterday when Marla gave me the camera."

Carol jumped on Kimberly's words. "Did Marla tell you the batteries had been recharged? Cause if she did —"

"No, no, she didn't actually say anything." Kimberly didn't want to give Carol any reason whatsoever to have a "friendly" talk with Marla. "I should have double- checked them myself yesterday when she gave them to me instead of assuming it had been done."

She turned to look at Marla but found Ricardo jogging up to them.

"Amiga, we're ready to shoot. You're supposed to be doing continuity," Ricardo said to her, in between a bit of huffing and puffing and a nod to Carol. "Greg is ready to go."

"Right," Kimberly said. "I'll be right there."

"What's the matter with you?" he asked, looking at Carol.

"What else? Isn't it always your grand diva over there?"

Ricardo looked at Kimberly. "What'd she do?"

"It's nothing. Just the battery thing."

Ricardo turned back to Carol. "What's that got to do with Marla?" he asked. "You don't..., no. Marla would not do such a thing."

"Oh, that's right, stick up for her."

"I'm not sticking up for her —"

"You're defending her —"

"Hey, guys, stop it," Kimberly said, trying to break up the argument.

Carol smiled sweetly at Ricardo. "I'll see you later?"

Kimberly wasn't fooled by Carol's smile; she doubted Ricardo was, either.

"Of course," he replied.

He looked as though he had more to say, but Marla's voice stopped him when she called for him. He made the mistake of waving back at Marla. When Kimberly saw his reaction to the look on Carol's face, she decided to step in.

"Let's meet up later, okay?" she said to him.

Ricardo nodded and didn't wait for Carol's reply. He obviously decided it was a cut-and-run moment. Kimberly didn't have to look at Carol to know she was mad. She could feel the heat emanating from her friend. Kimberly wished she had the guts to run, too. Carol had a real temper.

"Look at him," Carol said, still looking after Ricardo. "What is it with him and her? Can you believe he actually tried to defend her? Look at what he does. Every time she calls, he drops everything."

Kimberly had noticed the same thing; however she wasn't about to feed Carol's mounting jealousy. "I don't know, maybe he feels he has to answer because he works camera, and Greg needs him."

Carol pushed back a wayward swatch of purple-laced hair and turned back to her friend. "You know I don't trust Marla. She set you up. I know she did. I may not know how she did it but I know she did it."

Kimberly shrugged and picked up the script from the nearby chair. "Maybe, maybe not. I don't have any reason to say she did—"

"Ha! Why not jealousy? You saw her face yesterday when Mr. J called out your name. She was mad," Carol said.

"I know. She did look mad, but I'm not quite sure why. She's best friends with Greg, and she kept saying she'd rather act than play with the cameras," Kimberly said. She scanned the first pages of the script and noted that Marla was the centerpiece of the scene. Bad enough to have to look at Marla while wondering whether she'd tried to set Kimberly up for a fall with the battery problem, but now she'd have to listen to her take center stage the rest of the morning and follow her words line by line. What a thrill.

"Well, you can be nice if you want, but I'm telling you I wouldn't put anything past that girl," Carol said. "I got to go get some of the other actors ready."

"And now I have to go check continuity for Barry—"

"You mean you're going to have to watch Marla do her whole diva thing? Maybe you could trip her up—"

"No way," Kimberly said, trying not to laugh. "I'm not getting all worked up into some kind of revenge binge with Marla. Go do your make-up. It looks like they're ready to start."

"Yeah, okay, you just watch Miss Marla over there before she really gets you in trouble. I wouldn't turn my back on her,"

Carol reiterated and waved her long, manicured hand. "Don't you worry about continuity, girlfriend. You can handle it just fine. Trust me."

"I know, I know," Kimberly said, trying to placate her friend. "Right now I just want to let the whole battery thing go and focus on what's important."

With that, Kimberly left Carol and joined Ricardo, Greg and Marla by the stairwell for the first scene. As Marla said her first lines, Kimberly scanned the script and took in the setting, looking at every detail from Marla's moves to the position of the props nearby. She knew she'd have to remember it all so if something were amiss later she would be able to identify the potential problem. Every little thing had to match. If Marla or one of the other actors held a prop in a different hand than in a previous take, it could ruin an entire day's work.

Kimberly concentrated on the script. Luckily she had been able to recharge the second battery, so things calmed down and ran smoothly. Now and then she wondered if Greg was still harboring any of his earlier anger. Totally absorbed in his work, he hadn't said much to her.

The next scene required the actors to be involved in a chase sequence using the stairwell to the next two upper floors and would need intricate lighting. She focused on the quick tips Ricardo fed her as she helped him change out the lighting at Greg's gruff, monosyllabic directions. She pulled a lamp from a case and handed it to Ricardo, who perched precariously on a stool with one foot on the stair railing.

"Hand me the duct tape, will you, amiga?"

Kimberly leaned over the railing and eyed the dim stairwell as she handed him the tape. The chase scene would demand a great deal of lighting skill. There were few places to hang the lamps.

Greg adjusted the camera, walked to the stairwell, rechecked the positions for the lights, and finally muttered more directions to Ricardo before returning to the camera. She admired Greg's attention to details, a skill she had not mastered. She tended to "wing it" and rely on her artistic flair to get her through. She found the technical stuff boring and chased after the excitement generated by her style. So far, she'd been lucky. Her talent had never failed her.

"Hey, can you bring me another roll of tape?" Ricardo called.

Kimberly nodded and leaned forward. She and Greg collided as he reached for the same roll.

"Sorry," she muttered, rubbing her temple.

Greg smiled, a slightly crooked smile, as he handed her the tape. "I should be more aware of the world around me."

He'd removed his cap, and his hair had sprung into an unruly mass of curls and reminded Kimberly of a small boy whose wet hair had dried in the sun. His sudden warmth freed her of the morning's earlier tension, and she realized she liked Greg. Liked him a lot.

"Hey," Ricardo said, "do either one of you camera-junkies think you can pull yourself away from one another and hand me the tape?"

Kimberly jumped at the sound of Ricardo's voice. "Yeah, sure," she said and handed the roll to him.

"How many takes do you think we'll have to do on this sequence?" Ricardo asked as he smoothed the last bit of tape into place.

"Let's hope we can do it the first time around," Greg said. "I want to get up on the roof this morning."

Kimberly thought he was a bit optimistic.

Two hours and several retakes later, they were about to go up on the roof. Ricardo ambled toward Kimberly and lazily wrapped his arm around her shoulders. "You're doing just fine. Thanks for all the help earlier."

Kimberly nodded. "No problem."

"Hey, Greg liked that last angle you suggested."

She shrugged. "I thought it would make the scene a bit more dramatic during the close-up, that's all."

She sneaked a glance toward Greg, who had pulled his cap from his back pocket and put it back on, smashing flat all those wonderful curls. He and Barry were looking at the script and talking back and forth. She assumed it was about the next sequence of shots scheduled for the roof.

She decided to start gathering the equipment and get ready for the move.

Thirty minutes later the crew and the equipment littered the twelfth story roof. Mr. Jeffries had arrived to oversee everything. Despite the heat, Kimberly unpacked the equipment and readied the camera while Greg, Ricardo, Barry and Mr. Jeffries discussed the next plan of action. Within minutes beads of perspiration slipped down her face, neck and back. She envied Ricardo in his long, sleeveless muscle shirt. Grabbing a sandbag to weight the tripod, she felt another wet trickle run down her back and thought of Carol, who had stayed in the air-conditioned lobby. Smart girl, she thought and wiped her face.

Finally, she collapsed in a heap on the roof. She looked for something to shield her from the blinding sun. The scrim fit the job, and she held one over her head to block the sun. Greg appeared suddenly and dropped down next to her. He handed her an iced bottle of water.

"You look like you could use it," he said, smiling and taking control of the scrim.

Greg leaned behind her and moved the scrim against the back wall. As he did, his arm brushed against her back. She instinctively shifted toward him, then rolled the water bottle against her forehead in an effort to cool down.

Rising to his knees, Greg dug deep into his back jeans pocket. Kimberly had no idea what he was doing, but she wished he would sit down. She had become acutely aware of his presence. She smelled the woodsy cologne, heard his breathing, sensed his leaning closer and closer even as he dug deeper into his pocket.

A few seconds later he waved a bandana in the air, then shifted until he was behind her and wrapped the cloth band around her forehead. When he had finished, he continued kneeling behind her, his hands resting casually on her shoulders, and said, "That should help. This sun is intense."

That's not all, she thought. His breath whispered against her ear and cooled her cheek as he spoke. The warmth of his palms resting on her shoulders radiated more heat than the late morning sun burning her exposed sun. The soft, lingering scent reminded her of a cool, dew-drenched forest, mingled with the humid air between them.

Despite the awkwardness of the moment, she didn't move. She liked his touch, his scent, his attention.

A sharp whistle blast shattered the moment. Barry, in a hurry to finish the scenes on the roof, was trying to hustle everyone into action.

"Guess it's time," Greg said, his voice still soft.

She nodded. "Yes, we better go." She saw Barry waving for her to join him. "Barry calls."

Greg laughed and got to his feet. "At least he hasn't blasted us with his whistle."

When Greg left, she felt the loss. She couldn't sit around thinking about him, so she grabbed the script and jogged over to where Ricardo had set up the camera. Thanks to Barry, she had something else to keep her occupied. Barry had the actors do a number of retakes and Kimberly could see that Marla was getting tired. Maybe the heat was starting to get to her. It certainly was slowing Kimberly down.

During the last take, Kimberly started to think something was off, not quite right. She watched Marla pace in front of the camera, each step retracing the exact path she took before.

Despite her careful efforts, Kimberly couldn't figure out what was bugging her.

During a short break, Ricardo slipped next to her. "You sure are watching Marla. Don't tell me you want to be her understudy."

"Hardly," she said and shrugged. "I don't know. Something just doesn't feel right."

"You and Greg make a real pair. You both need to relax. Everything looks fine."

Shading her eyes, she looked across the roof. "Did you watch Marla do the crossover earlier?"

"Yeah, of course I did. Through the camera," he said and folded his arms across his chest. "Who wouldn't watch her make her moves? Did you see how her hair swings gently at the end as she takes a step?" Then his smile sagged. "You don't think Marla made a mistake, do you?"

Kimberly sighed. "I don't know. Maybe I'm trying too hard. You're probably right, and everything's fine." She glanced at Marla again and watched her throw her head forward then toss her long silky-red mane.

"She looks good to me, girl," Ricardo said and shifted his weight to get a better look at Marla. "She hardly ever makes a mistake; but, look, if you think there's a problem you need to tell Greg now."

She stood and replayed the last scene in her mind. She tried to visualize Marla's actions. Nothing. She still could not get it out of her head by the time Greg joined them.

"Looks like we're ready to break everything down, pack up and leave," he said, but his clear eyes shadowed when he looked at Kimberly and Ricardo. "What's the problem?"

CHAPTER SIX

W hat is the problem, Kimberly thought. Was there a problem? "I'm not sure—"

"If you noticed something, anything, now's the time to say so. We can easily do a retake," Greg said.

She turned and looked at Marla. Her hair glistened in the full sun. The image of Marla's curtain of hair draping forward during the last take slipped into place. "It's Marla—"

"Marla?" Greg said, surprise clearly evident in his voice.

"Yes, her hair, I'm sure it fell forward during the last take. In the earlier shots, her hair had hung straight down her back."

Greg digested her words before answering. From the lost, inward look on his face, she imagined he was replaying the last scene and calling up Marla's image. Then he was totally present and looked her in the eye before answering, "I think you're right. Help Ricardo set everything back up. I'll go get Barry and Marla."

With that, Greg left. Kimberly basked in a small self-congratulatory moment. Maybe this would make up for the earlier screw up with the batteries. Then she went to find Ricardo.

After the retake, they quickly dismantled the equipment and headed out to the garage to load everything into Greg's van. She was still smiling from the pats on the back she'd received from everyone, Mr. Jeffries on down, for the continuity call when

Ricardo came up and asked her if she planned to meet them at McDonald's.

"Tradition," he said as he hailed Carol. "We always pile into a McDonald's to review the day's work and load up. I don't know about you, but I'm famished. Donuts and coffee don't have much staying power."

Why not, she thought, starting to feel her stomach grumble.

On the way to the car, she remembered that Carol was still mad at Ricardo. She wondered if Carol planned to go to the restaurant. Apparently Carol was more interested in playing matchmaker because she'd already told Greg they'd be there. On the way, she peppered Kimberly about her morning with Greg. She wanted to know everything that happened, but Kimberly dodged the questions. She didn't want to talk about her feelings. She wasn't ready to share them with anyone.

Once at McDonald's they trooped through the doors and made for the bright yellow counter. Kimberly felt part of the group and loved it. The girl at the counter waited patiently while Greg and Ricardo went back and forth until they finally made a decision. Carol hung back and refused to talk to Ricardo. The rest of the cast and crew stumbled through the doors and got in line. The smell of grease, French fries, and burgers, assaulted Kimberly's nose as she listened to the back and forth between the workers calling off the orders from the drive-through.

"Give me two Homestyle burgers all the way, a large fry, and a hot apple pie," Ricardo said and looked at Carol. "What do you want? Coffee or Coke?"

Kimberly glanced at Carol, who was still mad. Clearly Ricardo hadn't gotten the message. Would Carol let it go? Kimberly had no idea.

"Diet Coke," Carol finally said.

Lunch might not be a total disaster, Kimberly thought, although she saw that Carol had not gone to stand next to Ricardo.

"Hey, what do you want?" Ricardo asked Kimberly.

"Just water and maybe a fried apple pie,"

Ricardo raised his eyebrows. "Hey Greg, a woman who is not watching her weight."

"Let her be," Greg said and put his arm around her, pulling her close. "Cheeseburger, large coffee, and fries for me."

A few minutes later, he handed her the water and took his coffee. "Let's go get a table."

Kimberly wasn't sure how to act. Greg's sudden move surprised her. She followed him to the booth. The smell of his coffee tickled her nose as she slipped past him and slid onto the bench. Greg settled in beside her. She watched Ricardo and Carol wait for their orders.

"You did a great job today," Greg said, tipping his coffee cup in a salute before taking a sip.'

"Thanks," she said and wondered if she should bring up the battery problem.

"I mean it. I'm glad you're working with us."

"Then you're not upset about Marla—"

"Marla? Heck no," he said, then popped a French fry into his mouth. "Don't get me wrong, I did want her. Hey, I've been working with her for years; we're friends. It would have been a comfortable fit, but you're doing great."

A huge knot inside Kimberly's stomach unraveled and all the tension, worry and concern she'd carried deep inside evaporated in an instant. "That's good to hear," she said.

Ricardo and Carol finally brought their food to the table, and everyone stayed quiet for a few minutes while they ate. Kimberly wondered if that was the only reason for Carol's silence. Minutes later Ricardo's hamburgers disappeared. Carol teased him about his humongous appetite and they all laughed. Now Kimberly could totally relax. It wasn't a lot of fun to be around Carol when her green-eyed monster ruled.

She finished her apple pie and listened to the chatter of the cast and crew around her. They all sounded excited when they talked about the morning's work. Ricardo and Greg talked about possible problems in upcoming shoots. Sitting there, Kimberly felt even more a part of the group. Even better, she felt closer to Greg. It had been a good day. When it was time to leave, Greg walked her to Carol's car and carefully shut the door once she was inside. His small wave echoed her own as Carol pulled away from McDonald's.

"So what do you think?" Carol asked, dividing her attention between the road and Kimberly. "Are you going to go out with him?"

Kimberly downplayed the morning. "Carol, he hasn't said a word about going out."

"Oh, come on, girlfriend, that boy is going to ask you out. I know. You'd be some kind of fool if you don't do it. I've been trying to get you two together, but it's so hard —"

"Why is it so hard?"

"Greg's got major responsibilities. He's got a younger sister and two younger brothers. His dad left the picture years ago, so Greg has to help his mother out. You know, watch the kids, take them for doctor visits, make runs to the mall, do the homework thing, all that stuff. But this intern thing will work out super. You'll be with him all the time. He's such a hottie. All the girls want to date him. You gotta go out with him, girlfriend. You'll be the envy of every girl at Northrupp."

Kimberly had to agree. Suddenly her junior year looked pretty good. Not only had she won the internship but it looked like she might win the boy. She smiled at the thought. By anyone's standards, Greg was worth winning.

* * *

Carol dropped Kimberly off at home and went on her way. Kimberly caught herself humming as she pushed open the kitchen side door and entered the house. She couldn't remember when she'd had such a good time and felt so happy — well, yes she could but today she absolutely knew no one could bring her down.

"Kimbo, where've you been?" Bobby asked, smiling. He sat at the kitchen table with a plate of homemade nachos and a large glass of iced tea. He was dousing the nachos with jalapeno pepper juice.

Kimberly brushed aside her irritation at the nickname and searched the kitchen for signs of her mother but didn't see her.

"I had to work on the video this morning."

"Mom said you needed some more driving practice before you take your test. She asked me to ride with you. Let me finish these," he said, pointing to the plate of nachos, "and I'll be ready to go."

"I'd rather wait for Mom."

"Come on, Sis, Mom's got some stuff she has to do. I can ride with you." Bobby popped two nachos into his mouth and took a swig of tea.

Her brother seemed genuine in his desire to have her help, but she didn't want him in the car with her. He always made her feel self-conscious. The last thing she needed was to be any more nervous than she already was when she was driving.

"I don't think so. I'd rather ride with Mom."

"Mom can't do it. If you want to practice today, you'll have to do it with me."

"Where's Mom?"

Her brother threw his cell phone at her. "Here, you call her."

Kimberly caught the phone, flipped it open, and hit the digits for her mother's cell phone number.

"Mom, Mom, this is Kimberly, can you hear me?" Her mother sounded like she was in a well. "I can't hear you. Where are you?"

Kimberly kept trying to talk to her mother, but half the messages were garbled. What she did get, though, was that her mother wanted her to practice and wanted her to do it with Bobby. She said goodbye and threw the phone back at her brother.

"I guess it's you today or I won't be getting my license Monday." She tried not to let her voice sound as bitter as she felt. She just didn't want Bobby with her. He always made her feel inferior, and she was nervous enough without him lurking about.

Her brother smiled and popped a nacho into his mouth. "I'll be ready in a few minutes."

"Fine. I'm going up to my room."

She left her brother in the kitchen and ran up the stairs to her bedroom. She tried not to let her anger get the best of her, but it wasn't easy. She wanted her license. She needed her license. She was so tired of having her mother or her dad take her everywhere. It didn't matter that she could do the driving. They were still in the car. She'd been so grateful when Carol got her license a month ago and started driving the two of them around.

Kimberly decided to change clothes and put on her khakis and a v-necked tee. Boy, was she wrong about her mood. Her brother had once again managed to ruin it for her. She reapplied her make-up. She just had to pass the test Monday.

From her bedroom, Kimberly heard Bobby yell that he was ready and heading out to the car. Kimberly ran down the stairs and into the garage. By the time she got there, Bobby had already started the car and scooted over so she could get behind the wheel. She backed carefully out of the driveway.

For the next hour, the two of them drove around the neighborhood, with Kimberly concentrating on her driving skills. After a while, she began to relax. Her brother tried to give her some good tips, and he didn't even tease her when she turned the corner too wide and had to swing back into the right lane. By the time they returned to the house, Kimberly felt a lot more confident. Of course, she wasn't about to tell that to her brother.

* * *

The rest of the weekend passed quickly. Kimberly spent most of the time in her room. She had to study for several tests. Monday morning she woke up confident and looked forward to taking the driver's test later that day. What she hadn't expected was that Bobby would be the one to go with her to the DPS for the big driving test.

Kimberly entered the DPS office and immediately searched for a place where her brother could sit and wait. Instead, she found a long line and chairs full of people. She took her place in line and begged her brother to see if he could find an empty chair somewhere, but he said he'd stand with her. She tried not to look at him or even talk to him, but Bobby made it hard with all his incessant questions. For some reason, he had decided this was the time to play catch-up with his little sister. All of a sudden, he wanted to know what she'd been doing, how the video project was coming along, what was Carol doing, and had Kimberly picked out a college yet.

Thank heavens he didn't know about Greg. She would just die if he ever found out about Greg. Bobby never could keep his mouth shut, and he teased her unmercifully. She couldn't figure out why he was so interested in her life. He never was before. He stayed up at college all the time, rarely came home, and she couldn't remember when they ever had a real talk. Not so with her mother. Every week her mother called Bobby and every week Kimberly had to listen to her mother give her the latest news flash on Bobby. Bobby this, Bobby that. Bobby, Bobby, Bobby. Her mother obsessed over Bobby.

Kimberly kept her eyes trained ahead and tried to ignore him. She hoped that if she didn't look at him he wouldn't start questioning her. She just wanted to focus on the upcoming test. She just had to pass.

CHAPTER SEVEN

Two hours later, her patience paid off. She was about to take her driving test. Thankfully, Bobby had finally conceded he was too much of a distraction and left her alone. She felt a rush of excitement. She found Bobby and grabbed the car keys. He simply smiled.

Once inside the car, Kimberly took a deep breath and turned the key. The officer guided her out of the parking lot and onto the street. "I'm a little nervous," she said and tried to stifle a giggle that pushed to the surface.

"Just do the best you can," the officer said. He directed her to turn here and there and occasionally marked the paper on his clipboard.

Finally, he guided her back to the parking lot. "All right, Miss," he said. "We'll add your score and see how you've done."

Kimberly waited in absolute agony. She did not want to fail. She couldn't stand any more days of being driven about by her mother, her father, Carol, or, worst of all, her brother. She so wanted to pass. Maybe a prayer would help.

"Well, Miss Lange, you've passed."

Kimberly shrieked and almost leaned over and gave him a kiss — but didn't.

"You can drive home if you like, Miss. Take this certificate inside and you'll receive your driver's licesnse."

Kimberly wanted to hit the pedal and drive out of there leaving Bobby in the dust. Instead, she drove the car around to the front of the DPS office, went inside, and turned in the piece of paper. A few minutes later she had her brand new driver's license. She couldn't help but smile. She even liked her photo. When she looked around for her brother, she saw him standing by the door, talking to a group of people sitting nearby.

"I'm driving," she said. "Enjoy the ride."

"Oh no," he said, putting on a face of mock horror and turning to the people waiting next to him. "They just licensed a new road hazard!"

Everyone laughed as they walked outside. It was just like Bobby to make friends so easily wherever he went without trying when Kimberly had to work so hard for everything. But even that annoyance couldn't dampen her excitement.

"I passed," she said, laughing and staring at the license. "This is so cool."

"You passed!"

Kimberly took her foot off the brake and headed the car for home. Wait until Carol hears about this, she thought. She'll love it.

"Hey," her brother said. "What do you think about the car?"

"The car?" she said. "This car?"

The car belonged to her brother. He'd driven it down from Austin. It was an okay sedan but nothing like what she hoped her dad would get her now that she had her license.

"You don't seem to be having any trouble driving it."

"Huh? Oh, none at all."

Kimberly didn't spend the rest of the short trip home thinking about all the fun she'd have now that she could drive. Finally, she'd have the freedom to go where she wanted, when she wanted.

Once home, she parked the car in the driveway and sailed into the kitchen. She saw her dad first. He'd already changed out of his suit and had put on his sweats. In a few minutes, he'd be out the door and doing his nightly run around the block.

"I did it," she yelled. "I did it."

He smiled and put down the paper he'd been reading. "I'm assuming that you passed the driving test?"

Kimberly ran up and gave him a big kiss on the cheek. "I did. I did. You should have seen me, Daddy. No problems. Right, Bobby?"

In a moment of absolute generosity, Kimberly had included her brother into the grand scheme of things. She was so happy even Bobby couldn't bring her down.

"She did great. You should have seen her drive us home." Bobby pulled a kitchen chair out and sat down. His fingers inched toward the cookies on the plate.

"You drove your brother's car?" her dad said. "What did you think about it?"

"No problems. Where's Mom?"

"Upstairs," her dad said.

He looked like he was about to say something else, but Kimberly couldn't wait. "I'm going to go tell Mom the good news. Isn't it great? You and Mom won't have to drive me around anymore."

She raced up the stairs and found her mother putting up the clean towels in the linen closet and shared her news. Then she ran back down the stairs and returned to the kitchen in time to overhear her brother and father talking.

"My car will be just fine for her. Why buy a new one when you can take over mine. I want a new car, and now I can afford one."

Kimberly stared at her brother. "What are you doing?" she screamed.

Her father jerked his head up and looked at her. "Honey, what's the matter?"

"Him," she said, pointing to Bobby. "He's the problem; he's always the problem."

Her mother rushed into the kitchen. "What's the matter? I heard you all the way upstairs?"

Bobby looked nonplussed. "I haven't got a clue."

"I don't want his car. I want my own car," Kimberly yelled and turned to Bobby. "You planned this all along. That's why you wanted to take me to get my driver's license —"

"Whoa, Sis, hold on. I'm just trying to help," Bobby said. "What's with the hysterics?"

"I'm not hysterical."

"Honey, you are a bit over the top," her dad said. He pulled out a chair. "Sit down and let's talk."

"No." She stood where she was and folded her arms across her chest. "I'm not going to talk about this. I don't want Bobby's car. Daddy, you promised me a car of my own when I got my license."

"Yes, — but your brother's offer is generous. We need to discuss this," her father said and patted the chair. "Sit down and let's talk it over."

Kimberly looked from her father to her mother. Seeing no help coming from her mother, she stormed out of the kitchen and took the stairs two steps at a time. How could Bobby push his way into her life and try to pawn his old car off on her? She slammed her bedroom door so hard the photographs bounced against the wall.

When she glanced at the computer, she saw an IM from Carol. Did she pass the test? Kimberly sat down and clicked away her message telling Carol all about her brother and his lousy effort to get rid of his car. She was still furious and telling Carol didn't make her anger any less.

After a few minutes, Carol IM'd her and suggested they go to the bookstore nearby and meet up with some of the kids. Kimberly agreed. A change of scenery would be good.

Her mother met her at the top of the stairs. "Kimberly, whatever's gotten into you?"

Kimberly instantly felt bad. Whatever she might be feeling because of Bobby, she shouldn't take it out on her mother. "I'm sorry. I just had my hopes pinned on the new car you and Daddy said you'd get for me when I got my license."

Her mother stroked her arm and gave her a kiss on the cheek. "Honey, I know but we didn't mean a brand new car. Bobby's offered to give you his car. We wouldn't have to pay for it."

Hearing her mother's words, Kimberly felt a sudden sense of shame flood through her felt even worse. "He's giving it to us for free?"

"He's giving it to you," her mother said.

"Oh."

"Why don't you go down and talk to your father?"

"Carol's on her way, we're going to the bookstore to study." She held up her book bag.

"Then talk to him when you get back."

Yes, she should have talked to her father. She knew that. But she hadn't thought Bobby would give her the car for free. She thought he was trying to find a way to take advantage of her wanting a car. So maybe she did over-react just a little bit. "Yeah, sure, Mom. Later." She started down the stairs and stopped. "You'll tell Daddy I'll talk to him when I get home?"

"Sure, honey. Sure."

Carol was already in the driveway when Kimberly opened the front door. She got in the car, and they headed for the bookstore.

"Isn't it great, Carol? I got my license."

'That is so awesome."

Kimberly settled into the car and pushed her book bag out of the way. "Yeah, I can't wait to start driving around. Now you won't have to cart me around everywhere."

Carol gave a little sideways glance toward her and then refocused on the road ahead. "I don't mind. I love driving you around."

"Yeah, I know, but this will be so much better."

Carol was silent the rest of the way to the bookstore. Kimberly didn't think too much about it because she was too engrossed in her own plans — driving plans.

When they got to the bookstore, Carol and Kimberly headed for the coffee shop and tables.

"Look, there's Greg," Kimberly said and nudged Carol. The two of them had lined up at the counter to make their order.

"I know," Carol said, laughing. "He and Ricardo got here earlier."

"He and Ricardo?"

"Yes, Greg said he wanted to meet up with you. I guess it's one of those rare days when he can get out of the house."

Kimberly could feel the rush of blood to her cheeks and knew she was turning red. "You didn't tell me," she said.

Carol grinned. "I know. I figured it would be a great surprise."

Vikk Simmons

CHAPTER EIGHT

G reg left his seat and came to stand next to Kimberly. She suddenly felt confused. What should she say? She never was good at this stuff. Carol didn't help with that smirky smile on her face.

"Hi," he said and touched her arm. "I hoped you'd make it."

The sound of his voice cushioned the empty place between them, adding warmth. The clatter and noise of the bookstore and the random movements of other students sitting at the tables and spread out along the floor between the bookshelves faded away. They stood alone, standing side by side, each knowing the other, discovering the other. She heard the sincerity in his voice; she felt the security in his touch. Thoughts of her earlier argument with her brother and father drifted away.

"Do you want whipped cream?" the girl at the counter asked.

Her voice cut through the space between them and separated them. Startled, Kimberly groped for words, any words. "Yeah, sure, whatever."

Carol turned and looked at her.

Kimberly shrugged. "Guess I wasn't paying attention."

"Neither was I," Greg said, his hand still hovering over her arm.

Acutely aware of his presence, Kimberly paid the girl and moved down toward the end of the counter. Greg followed.

Her emotions swirled like tiny whirlpools ready to pull her off balance. Surprised, she tried to concentrate, to engage her surroundings rather than fall into her internal chaos. The blast of the cappuccino machine caught her attention, and she watched the girl fill a cup with a thick layer of foam. She could almost feel the taste of the foam on her lips. Sighing, she turned away and sought her friend. Carol had already sat down at the table and was talking intently with Ricardo.

"I think they have a lot to talk about," Greg said, his voice barely a whisper brushing her ear.

"I think so," she said and stepped away to pick up her Café Mocha. She sipped it quickly, hoping to hide her awkwardness. She never knew what to do in these situations. Did she suggest they sit with Carol and Ricardo or should they find another table? Or maybe they should wander around the bookstore.

"There's a new book on directing, want to come with?" Greg said, answering Kimberly's unspoken questions.

She nodded, and the two walked away from the café and headed for the reference section where the books on writing were located. She didn't look back at Carol. She didn't want to give her a chance to change their direction — as if Carol would want to.

Greg found the book quickly. He put his drink on the shelf so he could scan the pages. Kimberly looked over his shoulder and tried to read, but he turned them too quickly.

"Wow, you can't be reading all that," she said and took another sip of her drink.

He laughed. "No, not in a thorough way but I have learned to speed-read a bit. It helps, enough to know if I want to buy it."

"Are you?"

He turned to face her and touched her hand. "Not a chance. You don't think I said that because I wanted to buy a book, do you?"

Kimberly's heart began thumping in quadruple time. He had only moved a little more than an inch closer, but the heat between them must have doubled. She looked away as if to catch her breath. "No, I guess not."

He picked up his drink. "Come on," he said and grabbed her free hand. As if she needed any more reason to follow.

He ushered her out of the book shelves and over to an empty table. He brushed what looked like muffin or cookie crumbs off the table and pulled out a chair for her. When she was settled in her chair, he sat down.

He was good looking, she thought, as the sun set behind them.

"Comfortable?" he asked.

"Fine," she said, noticing the strong, clean line of his chin that spoke to strength and character.

"Need a napkin?"

"No," she said. "I'm fine." She fought the urge to touch his hair, feel the curls. Her mind photographed and cataloged his features, enabling her to call them up at will at some future time. But when she came to his lips, soft and slightly full, she stopped.

"So how do you think we're doing so far?"

His words fell into the background as she imagined his lips touching hers.

"Kimberly?"

Startled, Kimberly realized that she had leaned forward. Before she could say anything or pull away, he caught her lips with his. She felt their softness.

Seconds later, they parted.

She held his gaze and saw lights in the silvered depths of his eyes.

"Nice," he said, the word sounding soft and warm.

CHAPTER NINE

Not too strong? Kimberly fought for control. Her emotions swirled, threatening to pull her off balance. The last thing she wanted was to fall into his lap. The depth and intensity of feeling surprised her.

"Kimberly?"

The sound of Greg's voice caused her to surface and break free from her emotional whirlpool. In the distance, she heard a sigh. Surprised, she realized it was hers.

"Maybe we should go and join Carol and Ricardo," Greg said and stood, holding out his hand.

She still hadn't caught her balance, and now he wanted her to stand? "Maybe we should."

As they walked back to the café, Kimberly remembered something she'd told Carol last year. She had sworn that she would never fall in love, never let anyone capture her heart. She had read somewhere—and she believed it — that an artist must choose between a life and a craft. Kimberly swore her life belonged to her craft.

What would Carol think if she could tap into Kimberly's emotional upheaval? For one brief moment, Kimberly felt as though she and Greg were one. Is that what everyone was talking about? Is that what true love does? All further thoughts were put on hold when she and Greg sat down at the table with Ricardo and Carol.

She felt the tension before she saw Carol's face. Then she knew. They were fighting.

"Fine, we'll ask Greg what he thinks," Ricardo said.

Carol put her hand on his arm and looked at Kimberly. "No, don't."

"No way. You think something's going on, so we need to talk about it."

Kimberly suddenly had a very bad feeling. She stared at the three diamond studs decorating one of Carol's ears and hoped against hope. She heard chairs scrape and the table next to them emptied of customers.

Ricardo ignored Carol's warning gesture and looked at Greg. "Carol thinks Marla set Kimberly up Saturday morning."

"What?" Greg started to laugh but must have realized Ricardo was serious. Greg leaned back to look more directly at Kimberly. "Marla? Set you up?"

His abrupt move caused a chasm that widened between them. Kimberly sought to close the gap. "No, I don't."

"Of course she does," Carol said, "and so does any reasonable human being that has an ounce of sense."

"Carol —"

"Why would Marla want to hurt Kimberly," Greg asked, his voice revealing his disbelief. Kimberly could tell he was struggling with Carol's accusation. "You know she didn't want the internship. I asked her to try for the position."

"Carol, shut up," Kimberly said, finally getting all the words out.

"What?" Carol said, surprise registering in her voice and on her face. "You know she did it."

"I don't," Kimberly said, answering Carol but keeping her eyes on Greg. "I just assumed — "

"Because of what Marla said," Carol said, interrupting Kimberly once again. "If she hadn't said she always charged the batteries you would have checked them."

Kimberly rose from her chair and stared down at her friend. Of all the times to start a war, she thought, couldn't Carol see something special had happened with Greg? "Will you please stop?" she asked, wishing Carol could read her mind.

"We need to discuss this now," Greg said. He looked from Kimberly to Carol, from Carol to Ricardo. "What do you know about this?" he asked his friend.

Ricardo shook his head. "Man, I don't know. It sure doesn't sound like Marla."

"Sure it does." Carol pulled her hand away from Ricardo.

"Chica —"

"Don't you chica-me," Carol said, her anger running like molten lava. "You're so captivated by that drama diva. How would you know what she's like?"

By now everyone in the café was looking at them, and Kimberly wanted to fade into the wallpaper. Several of the students sitting at the other table next to them were whispering and pointing at

Kimberly and laughing. Kimberly didn't know how to stop Carol's jealous rant.

"Carol, let's go. This isn't going to get any better," Kimberly said and pushed back her chair. She picked up her book bag and slung it over her shoulder. "We should go."

"No, wait," Greg said, touching her hand. "Do you really think Marla — "

"Oh, believe it." Carol stood so fast her chair slid back into the girl's chair sitting behind her.

Can we please leave now? Kimberly thought.

Ricardo stood. He looked lost. Like he didn't know what to say or do. Carol turned and left him there. She was out the door and on her way to the car before Kimberly had time to clear the table. She didn't know what to say to Greg, so she said nothing.

By the time she got to the car, Carol had already turned the key and had gunned the engine. Kimberly slid into the front seat and slammed the door. For the next ten minutes, they rode in silence. Kimberly finally tried to start a conversation, but was met with a hostile stare. Talking to Carol was useless when she was like this. When they finally reached her house, Kimberly slid out of the car and shut the door. She leaned down and looked in the car window but Carol kept her eyes facing front. She drove off without a backward look.

Luckily Kimberly didn't see any of her family when she went into the house and had no problems making it to her room. She dropped her book bag onto the end table by her bed, kicked off her shoes, and threw herself onto the bed. What was Carol thinking?

Thinking of Carol's awful behavior nearly caused Kimberly to forget what had happened earlier when she and Greg had gone outside — but not totally. Instantly Kimberly felt his lips on hers, remembered his hand resting on her arm, re-lived the swirling emotions that threatened to pull her down into herself. What a kisser, she thought. What a wonderful, wonderful kisser. She closed her eyes and abandoned herself to the memory.

CHAPTER TEN

K imberly woke up the next morning thinking about Greg. She wondered what he was doing, how he was feeling. She almost forgot that she had asked her brother for the keys to his — soon to be hers—car last night so she wouldn't have to ride with Carol to school in the morning. She'd also e-mailed Carol telling her she wouldn't need a ride. She had looked to see if Carol had replied. She hadn't, but Kimberly saw that the message had been read.

She knew she hadn't handled the whole thing with Carol very well, but the whole drama queen thing had finally been too much. Why did everything with Carol have to be so, well, large? She couldn't just suggest there might have been a miscommunication. No, she had to tell Greg that one of his best friends tried to sabotage Kimberly. Carol couldn't just ask Ricardo what was up with him and Marla. No, she had to blast him to hell and back about Kimberly's problem, and then she probably accused him of cheating with Marla. Carol seemed to end all her rage that way lately.

She and Carol had been best friends forever. All of a sudden their friendship was coming apart at the seams. When Kimberly had finally caught up with Carol at lunch, she tried to talk to her, but Carol snubbed her. Snubbed her. Kimberly couldn't believe her best friend in the whole wide world had snubbed her. What was the girl thinking?

Kimberly didn't know what to do, so she did nothing.

One day became two days and three days and still no Carol. Of course, Kimberly hadn't exactly gone up to her and tried to bury the hatchet, either. But it was Carol's fault, this whole thing. After all, she started it.

Thankfully, her job on the video project kept her away from Carol. Apparently make-up time in the cage had ended up with a knock-down drag-out with Marla refusing to sit in the chair and allow Carol to do her make-up. Carol, for her part, refused to look at Marla, let alone touch her. Kimberly had no idea how long this war would continue. Surely Carol would come to her senses soon.

The only good thing during the whole week was the time Kimberly spent with Greg. He called her every night; IM'd her whenever he was on the computer and pretty much occupied as much of her time as he could given his schedule. The more time she spent with him, the more she liked him.

As it happened, the more time she spent with Greg, the more she thought about Marla and wondered if Carol really wasn't misjudging her. Marla had only been nice since the day Carol had her outburst. In fact, Kimberly wasn't even sure Marla knew about Carol's accusations——at least she couldn't tell by the way Marla acted toward her. In the end, Kimberly decided Marla had simply forgotten to tell her the batteries needed charging. Besides, Kimberly should have double-checked them herself.

At the end of the second week, Mr. Jeffries decided the video project team members deserved a party. Barry had offered his parents' house for an overnight. Well, it wasn't a house. It was more a ranch. Barry told them there was a guest house with enough rooms for everyone and a big heated pool where they could party. The weather had been unusually warm, so everyone looked forward to the pool party. Mr. Jeffries handed out the permission slips and Kimberly had to do quite a bit of talking before her parents relented and allowed her to attend the overnight party.

When the big day arrived, Kimberly piled into the van with Greg, Ricardo, and Carol. Things were still awkward between Kimberly and Carol, but Kimberly vowed she would put her best face forward, and if Carol wanted to make up, she would be all for it. She was tired of fighting and tired of missing her friend.

By the time they reached the ranch, the sun limned the horizon and lights lined the trees along the driveway. Their sparkling glow matched Kimberly's anticipation as they pulled in front of the guest house. The cool evening breeze rustled the leaves, and the weeping willow branches teased her hair as she walked under its canopy. Greg walked alongside her, and Carol and Ricardo followed. Carol still hadn't talked to her, but Kimberly remained determined that she would have a good time whether Carol cooperated or not. When she heard a horse in a nearby paddock whinny, she paused to listen for an answering pounding of hooves. She loved the ranch already.

Her parents had finally consented to her going to the party when Mr. Jeffries called them and confirmed that he would be attending and that the boys would be housed in the bunkhouse. Of course, that meant that Kimberly would be under the same roof with Marla and with Carol.

Once in the guest house, the girls pounded up the stairs to the upper floor where the bedrooms lined the hallway. She watched Carol pick the first room and saw how she closed the door, closing off Kimberly, too. Then Marla ran into the master bedroom and claimed it——of course. The rest of the girls soon doubled and tripled up and claimed rooms. Marla had even invited two of the cast members to share the master bedroom. That left the smaller room at the end of the hall for Kimberly. She didn't mind. She liked being alone.

Kimberly unpacked quickly and had her clothes hanging in the closet and her suitcase empty and pushed under the bed in a matter of minutes. She had packed her Nikon on the slim hope that she'd be able to explore the ranch, and it looked like she'd have plenty of time before the party. She couldn't remember the last time she'd indulged her favorite pastime. She grabbed the camera and headed down the stairs and out the door. She stopped at the verandah and captured the view.

The scrape of footsteps startled her, and she jumped.

"Didn't mean to scare you," Greg said. His voice had softened and matched the quiet rustle of the country sounds. She heard a bird flutter through the branches while the resident cat stretched its body upward against a nearby tree trunk. Claws scraped the bark.

"Didn't hear you," she said.

"Care to sit?"

Kimberly joined him on the porch swing. He stretched his legs, and the swing creaked in response. "This is the life, isn't it?"

She allowed herself a moment to listen to the quiet. "Yes, I think so."

He ran his finger along the strap of her camera. "Nice one."

"Thanks. I like it." She relaxed, allowing the warmth generated by his closeness spread through her body. "Maybe you could come along while I take some photos?"

"Maybe," he said.

They continued to sit in the swing. After a little while, Greg stood and offered his hand. She accepted, and the swing creaked some more as she stood. Facing her, he brushed a wayward strand of her hair back behind her ear. "There, that's it," he said.

They remained silent, standing face to face. "Anybody ever tell you what great cheekbones you have?" he asked, touching her cheek.

His words rushed to fill the silent gap. "Really great."

She smiled.

He dropped his hand and stepped away. "We better go."

The two of them turned to leave the porch when the front door opened. Marla saw them and smiled. "Looks like you two are more than ready for the pool party."

Kimberly took in Marla's appearance and pushed down a stab of envy. The girl could wear a bikini. Marla had done her hair in a French braid and looked stunning. How could Greg resist her?

But Greg simply turned toward Kimberly and said, "Ah, pool party. I don't think I'm dressed correctly." He spread his hands open and stared down at his jeans.

Kimberly smiled. "I don't guess I am, either. Maybe we can do the photo shoot in the morning."

"Sure thing," he said turning to walk down the steps. Then he paused and looked back at her. "You are planning to have a good time, tonight?"

Kimberly simply smiled and walked past Marla into the house. The photos could wait.

A variety of old-style framed photographs stood on top of the bureau in Kimberly's room. She imagined they were images of past owners and visitors to the ranch, maybe some of Barry's immediate relatives. She made a note to ask Barry. She picked up an antique silver brush and stroked her hair. The sounds from the pool party drifted into the room from the open window. She never had the luxury of leaving a window open in the city. She resisted the urge to hurry, allowing herself extra time to manage her thoughts and emotions before seeing Greg again.

She had felt so close to him when they were on the verandah. She'd never experienced such closeness with anyone else, ever. She couldn't even remember when a boy had captivated her so. Of course, it didn't hurt that he had to be the cutest guy she'd ever been with, but that was beside the point. She had simply remained oblivious to anyone else's charms. Carol had called her a fool; Kimberly had called it being focused. She didn't have time for boys.

Now she felt divided. Her two selves, the promising cinematographer, and the blossoming woman vied for her attention. Instead of the camera being her main focus, the man behind the camera became the object of her attention. Her emotions confused her. She loved working so closely with Greg. They shared the same space, the same language, the same vision. Further thoughts evaporated when the splash of water and gusts of laughter drifted through the open window. She put the brush down. Dimming the lights, she left the room for the party outside —and Greg.

CHAPTER ELEVEN

By the time Kimberly arrived, the pool party was in full swing. Ricardo led the pack with wolf whistles as she approached. Carol had already joined the party. She'd dyed the swatch of hair green instead of purple, and her black bathing suit was adorned with studs and crosses, Goth-style. Kimberly doubted she'd be picked for Carol's team, so she walked slowly and scanned the crowd for Greg. He was already in the water, with Marla, of course. She slipped off her sandals, grabbed a towel and headed for his side of the pool.

Carol called out and claimed her as a player. Surprised, Kimberly stood at the edge of the pool and looked back and forth between Greg and Carol. Finally, she shrugged and jumped into the water on the side of Carol's team.

The game was fast and furious, and Kimberly soon forgot their friendship had ever been interrupted. They called out to one another, and she easily set Carol up for several good scores. At one point, she and Greg, who was on the other team, batted the ball back and forth over the net for at least five shot. Kimberly had to admit she felt a great deal of satisfaction when Greg missed the last slam.

"Hey, that was great," Carol said and bounced up and down in the water as she hopped toward Kimberly.

"Uh, yeah, thanks," Kimberly said. She wasn't sure if Carol was ready to make peace yet but if she was, Kimberly was all for it. She didn't like warring with anyone.

"I'm glad you're on my team," Carol said, continuing to move closer.

"Yeah, me, too."

"Friends?"

Surprised by Carol's mercurial change in attitude, Kimberly still readily agreed. "We've never been anything else."

Carol smiled and gave her a hug.

Just then, Ricardo batted the ball straight at Carol, hitting her on the side of the head. When he saw what he'd done and that she wasn't hurt, he laughed and said, "Oops."

"Oops you," Carol said and dove into the water straight at Ricardo.

Ricardo dove away from the speeding Carol. Apparently the two of them had made up big time. Kimberly headed towards the pool ladder. Then she realized Greg stood at the side of the pool next to Marla. As Kimberly approached, he reached down to pull her up. He nearly lost his grip but grabbed her around the waist and pulled her in close.

'Hey, you're not getting away that easy," he said.

Kimberly grinned and, once she was on solid ground, pushed him away. "Oh yeah?"

Marla, who looked stunning in her emerald green bikini, and had moved in closer to Greg, laughed at them. "You two deserve each other," she said and pushed him toward Kimberly.

Greg caught her. "Don't think I'm going to let go this time."

Kimberly watched Marla glide away. "No, don't," she said. Then added, "She's all right."

Greg smiled and pulled her even closer. She felt his fingers moving against her skin, their heat burning her. "She is," he said. "I think a lot of people misjudge her, thinking she's stuck up and all but she's not. She's great."

Kimberly nodded. And so are you, she thought.

By then Greg had released her and had started toweling off. When he'd finished, he gave her his towel. She wrapped it around her waist, and the two of them wandered over to the table loaded with food. After they had downed a plate full of nachos and had their fill of soda, Greg suggested they walk around and see more of the ranch. He grabbed her hand, and they strolled away from the pool, toward the long drive that connected the guest house to the main house and toward the barns.

Moonlight lit the path and the soft midnight sounds of the paddocks bid for their ears. A comfortable silence fell into place between them. For the first time, Kimberly wondered if she'd been wrong to give up so much of her time to the pursuit of her dreams. Perhaps she'd been cutting herself short by not dating more. Had she been missing out?

When they reached the barn, Greg led her to the fence where he stepped onto the first rung, leaned over, and whistled. Suddenly a miniature horse appeared out of nowhere and nuzzled his hand.

"She knows I have sugar," he said and pulled a cube out of his pocket.

Kimberly joined him on the fence and leaned forward. Greg dropped a sugar cube in her outstretched hand, and she left her palm extended toward the horse. In seconds, he nuzzled her palm.

When a loud screech cut through the air and startled her, she lost her balance, slipping on the railing, and fell —not to the ground but into Greg's waiting arms.

She felt his arms encircle her. Her head fell against his still damp chest.

Another screech split the air. She pushed away from him. "What is that?"

Greg laughed. "That's Amos."

"Amos?"

"Amos the peacock, he's one of Barry's pets."

A dark shape moved in the trees above and, as Kimberly's eyes adjusted to the deep shadows, she began to see the long tail feathers and the dark crest. "Sounds more like a Banshee from Hell," she muttered.

"He has his moments."

Greg turned and headed back to the ranch house. He laid his arm lightly around her shoulders as they ducked under a willow branch, splaying its leaves like a fragile curtain. "Amos roosts in the tree branching over the guest house. If you're lucky, he'll give you a wake-up call."

"I can hardly wait," she said, although her thoughts were not on the noisy bird, but on the feelings engendered by Greg's touch. Beneath the delicate drape of the willow leaves, she felt she and

Greg stood alone touched only by the warm breeze. Did he feel the same magic when they touched?

Laughter rippled through the night air, shifting her thoughts back to reality. Greg pushed aside the willow leaves, and they continued. When they reached the pool, they found the cast and crew drawn into a loose circle around Barry. He was regaling them with his latest stand up comedy routine.

Greg had drawn Kimberly closer as they stopped by a nearby tree. His arm rested comfortably around her waist, and she naturally fell against him. She saw Marla standing in the shadows alone. Did he compare her waist against Marla's tiny one? Kimberly banished the thought. She would not give in to stupid thoughts like that. Greg was with her, not Marla. His quiet laughter caressed her ear as his touch teased her skin and his light woodsy cologne tickled her nose. He had slipped his thumb under her bikini strap on top of her shoulder and rubbed her bare skin back and forth.

Soft laughs interrupted the rhythmical sound of Greg's breathing. She felt his chest rise and fall in response to the laughter. Under the soft glow of patio lamps, his laugh lines deepened around his eyes. She looked into his eyes and the laughter faded into the night. Once more Kimberly felt them merge.

Greg caressed her face, and she closed her eyes. His breath warmed her, his lips answered hers. Everything disappeared as she gave in once more to the magical moment. Swirling energy seemed to lift her on her toes as she gave into his embrace.

He moved his hands up and down her back, warming and caressing her. His lips worked softly against hers, tasting and beckoning. When he pulled his body closer, she felt a sharp trill tunnel through her. She lifted her arms and placed them around his neck.

His lips still against hers, he said, "So this is what it feels like to have a life apart from school and work. If I'd known———"

A single, loud shriek blasted through the air, splitting them apart. Kimberly dropped her hands, smoothed the towel wrapped around her waist. "Amos," she muttered.

Greg shook his head and stepped away from the tree.

Kimberly searched his face and wondered if they were moving too fast. Her unease disappeared when she saw him smile.

"Think we could get Ricardo to bag the bird?" he asked.

"Maybe Barry would add barbecued peacock to the campfire menu in the morning."

Greg laughed. He then offered her his arm and escorted her to the guest house.

"I guess I'll see you in the morning?" she asked, trying to ignore the awkwardness of the moment.

"Most definitely," he answered, then leaned forward and gave her a quick peck on the cheek. "I'll see you———early in the morning," he whispered.

Kimberly stood on the verandah and watched him cross over to the bunkhouse. She still felt his touch on her cheek and carried the warmth of his voice in her memory. She wondered if she was falling in love.

The screen door squealed as she pulled it open, but a louder shriek ripped through the night. Kimberly let the door close and leaned over the porch railing. She searched the overhanging branches of a nearby tree. Sure enough, Amos had taken roost overhead, and it looked as though he had settled right over her room.

Cloaked in thoughts of Greg, Kimberly remained oblivious to the world as she glided toward her small bedroom at the end of the hall. She picked up her nightgown and went to the bathroom to change. When she returned, she found Carol sitting on her bed. She still wore her black two-piece bathing suit.

. "Hi," she said, unsure of what Carol might want. Although Carol had seemed to bury the hatchet, Kimberly wasn't sure how their relationship would continue given Carol's long silence the past couple of weeks.

"Looks like you and Greg are a definite hot item."

Kimberly couldn't stop the immediate smile that seemed to appear at the mention of Greg's name. "Yeah, I guess so."

"That's nice."

Carol's voice rang a trifle hollow on that one, Kimberly thought.

"How are things between you and Marla?" she said as she tweaked her spiked hair. "Any more problems?"

"No, none that I know of."

"I haven't seen much of you——"

"You know why."

"Guess you don't need me to drive you around anymore since you got your license."

Kimberly couldn't believe it. Carol all but accused her of being a shallow friend who only wanted Carol around when she could use her for her wheels. "That's not why."

Carol shrugged.

"Carol, have you gone Alzheimer on me? Don't you remember all that mess with Ricardo and Marla and me? You told Greg I blamed Marla for the battery problem."

"I've gone Alzheimer? That's a laugh. I don't believe I've seen you since you got your driver's license."

Kimberly jumped out of bed. "That's ridiculous. You're the one who was so hot to drive me everywhere when you got your license. I was a great excuse for you to get the car."

"Was not."

"Was, too. You said your mom didn't want to give you the car half the time, she always gave in when you told her I needed a ride. You'd have never made half the mall trips if I hadn't been there needing a ride."

"You are so ridiculous," Carol said, her words taking on a short staccato cadence. "You know Ricardo had the hots for Marla yet you did nothing about it."

"What are you talking about? Ricardo and Marla? That's insane."

"Don't bother denying it. You're still covering for him. I don't even know why I thought we could still be friends."

Then Carol did her big finale and stomped out of the room. She left Kimberly standing in the middle of the room and staring after her.

What was that all about? Kimberly wondered.

A slammed door answered her.

Kimberly tried to forget what had just happened, but it proved impossible. Her best friend had just gone mental, and she had no idea why. Who would have thought that getting her driver's license and getting a boyfriend could cause so much trouble?

Unable to sleep, Kimberly padded down the hallway, down the stairs and into the kitchen. She opened the refrigerator and searched the contents. She didn't find one piece of chocolate. Finally, she pulled out the bottle of milk and poured some into a super-sized mug. She microwaved the milk in hopes that hot milk would help her sleep, but she had a feeling the milk would not cure her problem. The problem was Carol.

Actually, the problem was Kimberly's feelings for Carol. She still considered Carol her best friend and she couldn't understand what was going on with her. Her jealousy seemed to touch everything, and the two of them couldn't be near one another without World War III erupting.

Kimberly slid onto a bar stool and stared into the mug of milk. Deep in thought, she nearly tumbled off the bar stool when Marla asked her what she was doing.

"Nothing," Kimberly said and took another swig of milk.

Marla gave her another one of her long looks. "I don't think so. You look like you lost your best friend——literally."

Kimberly tried to stop the sigh but failed. "Okay, yes, I've lost my best friend—— again."

Marla tightened the silk sash holding her robe closed and poured herself a mug of milk. "Mind if I share," she said and held the mug high.

Kimberly let a small smile slip by. "Sure."

The two of them listened in silence as the microwave hummed. "I'm sorry you're having such a hard time." When she saw Kimberly's questioning look, she added, "Your girlfriend wasn't exactly quiet earlier."

"Yeah, I guess she wasn't." Kimberly figured the whole guest house must have heard them argue, maybe even those in the bunkhouse heard. At that thought, Kimberly felt her mood grow even darker. Why did she argue back? After all these years, she knew not to engage Carol when she was like this. It would have been so much easier just to let her have her say and then try and talk to her in the morning.

"I guess it can be rough, being best friends and all," Marla said, still sipping her milk.

Surprised, Kimberly glanced at Marla. Surely she had a best friend. "Sure, you know how it is."

Marla stayed quiet.

Kimberly felt the silence grow awkward. "You do have a best friend, don't you?" Kimberly was trying to remember if she'd seen Marla with any one of the girls at school more than others. She hadn't. In fact, she hadn't seen Marla hanging with the girls at all. Did the girl have any real friends other than the guys?

"I have friends. Greg's always been there when I needed him...so has Ricardo."

"What about girlfriends?"

Marla sipped her milk.

"You must have at least one girlfriend. Who'd you hang with? "

Marla gave a slight shrug. "No one."

Kimberly stared at her. "Wow." Now that was an amazing thing to hear. "I can't believe that."

Marla looked up and stared into Kimberly's eyes. "Believe it."

Silence settled between them. Kimberly remembered all the years she and Carol had spent together and what good times they'd had. She couldn't imagine growing up without a girlfriend, let alone a best friend. To think she had envied Marla.

As if reading her thoughts, Marla continued. "I don't know why, I guess it's because of my looks, maybe even my personality or because I model and act. I don't know. It's easier and more comfortable to be with the guys."

She shifted and seemed uncomfortable, and Kimberly wanted to put her at ease. "Hey, I bet there are tons of girls who are just like you. Well, maybe not just like you, but they probably have the same problem trying to get a girlfriend who is as close to them as Carol has been to me."

Marla went to the refrigerator. She looked inside and pulled out a plate. "Look what I found at the back, behind the orange juice carton."

Kimberly strained to see what was in Marla's hand and smiled when she realized she had found a big, fat piece of what looked to be German chocolate cake with two big cherries on top. "Well, girlfriend, I think you've hit pay dirt. Bring that puppy on over here."

Marla smiled. Within seconds, she had divided the cake in two, pulled two forks out of the silverware drawer, and placed the divided pieces of cake smack in the center between the two of them. Without another word, she offered Kimberly a fork.

CHAPTER TWELVE

Kimberly licked chocolate icing from her fingertips. Nothing bonds girlfriends faster than chocolate, she thought. It was her one life-affirming rule. When in doubt, go for the chocolate. It's the answer to all of life's pesky questions. Chocolate certainly seemed to be the glue that bonded her with Marla. By the time they'd finished peeling every last ounce of chocolate off their plates, they had shared jokes, dreams, memories, and desires. Greg had been right about Marla all along. She really was a cool person and seemed perfectly capable of being a good friend, too.

She'd misjudged Marla. All she'd known of Marla was that of the girl seen through Carol's prism, and that prism, Kimberly knew instinctively, had been tinged pure green with envy and jealousy. Marla had no intentions on Ricardo. She didn't seem to have any desires for Greg, although she, too, agreed that he was a hottie. He just wasn't her hottie — and Kimberly was more than fine with that.

The two put out the kitchen lights and tip-toed to their rooms, each promising to help the other out and trying to suppress their giggles all the way up the staircase. Marla had to be especially quiet as she had two roommates. Kimberly left her at the master bedroom door and finished her stealth walk to the last bedroom where she carefully slipped into the room without making a creak or a squeal.

Not so Amos. He let out a shriek trumpeting to the world Kimberly's late arrival. Thankfully, no one seemed to hear.

The next morning Kimberly awoke to a late breakfast cooking downstairs. When she finally wrapped herself in a robe and wandered down the stairs, she thought she'd find all the girls in the kitchen, but only Marla stood over the stove, cooking bacon. She had turned and waved a hello when Kimberly appeared.

"What's up?" Kimberly asked. "Where is everyone?"

"I don't know. The place was empty when I got up." She flipped several strips of bacon, and the grease sputtered. "I guess everyone else got to sleep early."

Kimberly smiled at the memory of chocolate and cherries last night. "Yeah, I guess so." She sat on a barstool and tried to stifle a yawn. "What time did we call it a night?"

"Oh, about three or four," Marla answered. She piled the bacon onto a paper towel and began cracking eggs. "I assumed bacon and eggs would be good for you?"

"Sure, and coffee."

"Great."

Kimberly woke up enough to realize she should offer to help Marla out. "What can I do? Make the coffee, toast the bread?"

"No, no, sit yourself down. This won't be a minute. Besides, I do this all the time at home."

Kimberly understood. Marla lived at home with her dad. Her mom had died more than five years earlier and since then it had been just the two of them.

"This is fun for me," she said. "Really."

108

"Okay, girlfriend, it's your kitchen. Kimberly gladly gave up the breakfast to Marla.

"I don't know what's going on between you two, but Carol seems to be really angry——or maybe it's with me. She took one look at me this morning and stormed out of here."

"I guess she's still angry over our argument last night."

Marla brought the full plate of bacon and eggs over and slid it in front of Kimberly. "I'm sorry. I know she's your best friend."

A sigh slipped, and Kimberly said, "Yeah, she is—was—has been. I don't know anymore what's going on with her."

"I hope you two can patch it up."

"So do I."

Marla gave Kimberly a wistful smile. "It's too bad you can't convince her of my lack of interest in Ricardo — as a boyfriend. He's a great friend, one of the best, but he's not boyfriend material for me."

"I know," Kimberly said and pushed a strip of bacon around the plate. "I'll give it a try but I can't promise anything. Sometimes Carol refuses to take off the blinders."

Kimberly spent the rest of the morning getting dressed and packing. The bus Mr. Jeffries had arranged for was scheduled to leave the ranch at three, so she had barely an hour or two left. She wondered what Carol was doing but then decided to forget her. She didn't want to ruin any more of the trip. When she finally found Greg, she discovered that he, Ricardo and Barry had been working on the video script. She felt slightly out of the loop but then decided it was too nice a day to be mad. After all, she did stay up most of the night talking to Marla. When Greg heard the news of her and Marla's blossoming friendship, he couldn't have been happier- -and that made Kimberly happy.

Toward the end of the time at the ranch, Kimberly did finally make an effort to look for Carol. She finally found her sitting by the pool and alone. She thought she'd try again to reestablish their bond.

She stopped at the foot of the chaise and looked down at Carol. "Hi."

Carol lifted the magazine from her eyes and stared at her.

"I thought maybe we could talk."

Carol let the magazine fall flat, blocking the sun and effectively blocking out Kimberly.

Well, she thought, that didn't work out. "You know how to get in touch. If you want to talk or try to work this out, call me or find me."

Carol still didn't answer, so Kimberly left her lying in the sun, alone.

* * *

By the time Kimberly got to school on Monday, she'd put her anger toward Carol away. She didn't like the way it made her feel. She still didn't understand why Carol had turned on her. She didn't get it at all.

The only thing she could do was go forward, and that was exactly what she had determined to do. Marla met her in the hallway and asked her how it was going and seemed genuinely sorry that Kimberly hadn't been able to patch things up with Carol.

The trouble began in the cafeteria at lunch. As soon as Kimberly entered the room, she noticed a decided change in the attitude of some of her friends. A few turned away when she looked at them, others simply seemed to ignore her when she tried to join in their conversations. She stood in line, by herself, and filled her tray with the usual Monday fare: Macaroni and cheese, broccoli and a piece of apple pie.

The line moved fast and soon she stood in front of Mrs. Hemple, the cashier.

"Two-fifty," she said and held out her hand.

Kimberly gave her a five and waited for change. Behind her, she heard some chattering and mixed whispers. She turned to look, but the talk stopped.

Mrs. Hemple dropped the change into her outstretched palm, and Kimberly picked up her tray and moved on. She searched the cafeteria for a place to sit.

She started toward the table where a few of her homeroom friends sat, but they turned away when she approached them. Rebuffed, Kimberly continued to look for a place to sit. She finally saw Carol over at a table on the left side of the room. Carol apparently saw her at the same time because she turned toward the girls at the table and said something they found funny. Then she pointed toward Kimberly.

A hot flash flamed her face as Kimberly realized something was going on and that something was about her. She felt everyone's eyes on her. Well, maybe not everyone but it sure felt like everyone. She didn't know where to sit. She turned away from Carol's prying eyes and looked for the closest, empty table she could find and slid her tray onto the table. She had no idea why she was being shunned but shunned it was. All she wanted to do was run, but she knew she couldn't give Carol that satisfaction. It was bad enough for her to know she'd managed to make Kimberly's life absolutely miserable during lunch. Kimberly shoveled her food into her mouth and tried to finish as quickly as possible.

The rest of the day didn't go much better. By the end of sixth period, Kimberly was ready to go home. She tossed her books into her locker and slammed it shut. She couldn't wait to get away from school.

She had just reached her car when she heard someone running behind her. When she turned, still hoping it would be Carol ready to explain what was going on, she saw Marla.

"Hey, I've been trying to find you all day."

Kimberly opened her car door and tossed her book bag into the front passenger's seat. "I've been here——all day. Not that anyone cares."

"I'm sorry. I heard about lunch."

Kimberly couldn't have heard anything worse. Now Marla pitied her. Probably the entire school pitied her——at least those who weren't mad at her for whatever. "It's nothing. I survived."

"Look, Kimberly, I don't know what's going on but Carol's got it in for you. I hope it's not my fault."

Kimberly saw the look on Marla's face and knew she meant what she said. "You had nothing to do with it."

The girl's face relaxed into a partial smile. "Are you sure?"

"Sure I'm sure." Kimberly didn't think she was that sure, but she wasn't about to dump everything on Marla. The girl had enough problems dealing with everyone at school without making her a scapegoat for Kimberly's problems.

"Great." Marla continued to stare at her. She looked like she wanted to say something but didn't.

"What?"

"I don't know. I just thought maybe you'd like to come to my house?"

It took a lot for Marla to make the offer, but it wasn't the right time. Kimberly just didn't feel like socializing with anyone right now. Right now, she had one too many friends who seemed to have become enemies. Why try for more. "Look, I think I had better go on home," she said but was instantly sorry when she saw the look on Marla's face. "I'm sorry. I do have to go. My brother is going to go back to Austin any day. I should spend some time with him."

Marla seemed to perk up at Kimberly's excuse and said she understood. She left Kimberly alone in the parking lot, still wondering what the heck was going on with everyone.

And then, to make matters worse, she realized she hadn't seen Greg all day.

CHAPTER THIRTEEN

K imberly stood at the back of the visual arts room and cleaned camera lenses. The room was rimmed with movie posters and quotes about screenwriting and filmmaking. It had been two days since the disastrous lunchroom scene, and Kimberly still had no idea what was going on. What she did know is that she had become the school pariah. Carol had effectively cut her off from her friends in homeroom and gym class. Only Marla seemed to stand the test and stand with her. Not that that made her any more friends. Marla's pariah rating seemed to compete with Kimberly's for total isolation.

She looked around the room and allowed herself to relax. No one would be coming in right now. She had the place to herself.

Kimberly continued to busy herself with the equipment. Engrossed in what she was doing, she failed to hear the door open. When she did hear something, she turned to find Mr. Leonard, the school's principal, standing behind her.

"Ah-h-h, Kimberly, how's it going?" he asked as he looked over her shoulder at all the camera equipment.

She put the lenses away and faced him. "Fine, we're doing fine."

She wondered what he was doing there. She didn't know him very well. He never dropped in on video club, and he cared more about the sports program. At least he never cut the visual arts program.

"Have you seen Mr. Jeffries or even Greg Winters?" he asked.

What could he want with Greg? "Uh, no, I haven't seen either one this afternoon. Is there something I can do for you?"

Mr. Leonard seemed lost in thought for a moment, and then he brightened. "Yes, there is. As you know, the senior video project deadline is next week —"

"Yes, and we're right on track."

"Um, don't interrupt, please. That is the deadline for the project, but I'd like to know how close you are to finishing."

Kimberly stared. "Finishing?"

Mr. Leonard waited.

"Well," she began, and then she saw Greg's storyboard pinned on the corkboard. She waved him over to the storyboard. "As you can see, Greg has us on a tight schedule right until the final days before the deadline."

Mr. Leonard peered at the storyboard. Kimberly wasn't sure he even understood what it was, let alone what it meant. "Kimberly, this will not do."

"What do you mean?"

He pushed his glasses higher up his nose. "You do know we're having the annual banquet Saturday night?"

"Sure. Everyone knows that."

The principal paced back and forth in front of the storyboard. "This," he said, waving at the last segment. "It won't do. You must finish the video and have it ready to show the night of the banquet."

Kimberly couldn't believe her ears. The principal wanted the video to be finished, edited, completely done and ready to go in three days? He had to be on something, she thought, but said, "Uh, I don't think that's going to happen, sir."

"Why not?"

She fidgeted, shifting from foot to foot. What he was asking was impossible. Greg's storyboard set the schedule, and it would take a miracle——or at least a whole lot of rewriting and editing——to come anywhere close to what Mr. Leonard wanted.

"We, we just can't do that. It's impossible. Look, here, Greg doesn't even have us shoot the final scene until Friday morning."

"So," Mr. Leonard said. "That means you'll be done shooting and can show the film the next night."

"Video, sir, not film, and no that doesn't mean we're finished. It just means we've finished shooting, and all the acting and stuff is done. There's still an entire week of editing blocked out," she finished and pointed to the next week's schedule.

The principal peered at the board again. "Oh, you can do it. I know you can."

"I can't, Mr. Leonard. This is the senior video project. You need to speak to Greg."

"Kimberly Lange, don't tell me you can't do this. Mr. Jeffries spoke in glowing terms about you, your talent, and your capabilities. You can make this happen."

"I don't mean I can't, sir. I mean I'm not in the position to make any decisions or guarantee any final product." Kimberly did not like the way the conversation had suddenly turned. She needed to back it up fast.

The principal just looked at her. "Are you telling me you won't?"

"No sir, I mean, I just think you have to talk to Mr. Jeffries and to Greg."

The principal put his hands on his hips and looked around the room, and Kimberly couldn't help but wonder if he was this much of a pain every day. She was glad she never worked in the office. "Where are they?"

Exasperated, Kimberly said, "They're not here right now. I mean you need to take all this up with them."

"I don't have time for all that. I need an answer now." He leaned forward and pretty much stared her down. "Will you or won't you guarantee this film Saturday? If you have to talk to Mr. Jeffries or Greg, fine. But I want you to get this project done in time for the banquet Saturday night."

Mr. Leonard had her backed into a corner. He wanted the film Saturday. In her heart, Kimberly knew she could make some changes here and there to the script and the shooting schedule. They'd have to step up the work, but it was possible to have it done and ready to show in time to meet his deadline, but — BUT it wasn't up to her. And she didn't think Mr. Jeffries and especially Greg would put their stamp of approval on her ideas. It just wasn't up to her.

"I'm waiting," he said and scanned the storyboard once more. "Will you make this happen?"

"I don't have the authority."

"This is important for the school," he said and looked around the room, "and for all of you in the visual art program. We have a lot of alumni and benefactors who come to this banquet. They can fund a lot of the things we need. Take that new camera the school received —"

"We're using it for the video project, and Mr. Jeffries thinks the new camera will give us an edge." She regretted the words the minute they flew out of her mouth.

Mr. Leonard pounced. "Exactly my point. We need to show these people what the visual arts department is doing. The senior project is the best way."

"You should talk to Mr. Jeffries."

"Kimberly, I've heard you are a whiz at this video stuff. Mr. Jeffries showed me your application, including that short tape you included. He spoke highly of you. I'm sure you know whether what I'm asking is reasonable."

Mr. Jeffries bragged about her work to the principal. Kimberly couldn't help but feel good. She knew she had the talent. Now Mr. Leonard was telling her Mr. Jeffries confirmed it. "Well, thank you," she said. She stared at the storyboard. "It's a long shot, but I may see a way that it could be done. I could suggest a way —"

"Perfect, go ahead and get started. I'll talk to Mr. Jeffries later and tell him you have it all worked out." Mr. Leonard headed for the door. "This is great. I knew I could count on you."

"No, wait, that's not what I said." But Mr. Leonard had left the room. What had she done? She didn't mean she could definitely deliver the video. If the principal tells Mr. Jeffries and Greg that she guaranteed she could deliver, Kimberly knew they'd be angry.

That's what I get for running my mouth and trying to do things that don't concern me, she thought. She had no business even suggesting to the principal that there was a way. She should have held her ground and insisted he speak to Mr. Jeffries. But no, she fell for his flattery and stepped right in it.

Kimberly dropped into a nearby chair and wondered how she would try to convince Mr. Jeffries and Greg that it was possible to deliver the video by Saturday night. What was she going to say to Greg? What would he say to her?

CHAPTER FOURTEEN

By the time Kimberly got home, she still hadn't figured out a good way to tell Mr. Jeffries and Greg what Mr. Leonard wanted and that she had suggested a way to make it happen. She had to talk to them before Mr. Leonard did. She had to explain. Luckily her mother had left a note saying she had gone shopping, so Kimberly could plan on having a few moments of peace. She climbed the stairs to her room and threw herself on her bed. She couldn't believe Mr. Leonard said she'd have the entire video ready for Saturday night's banquet.

She didn't even want to think about what Greg would say when she told him. It was going to be hard enough to tell Mr. Jeffries. Kimberly felt a sharp pain in her stomach. Serves me right, she thought and ran to the bathroom.

A few minutes later, she heard her brother's voice. Not now, she thought. He's the last one I need to deal with.

"Hey, where are you?"

She heard Bobby bang on her bedroom door. She'd have to answer him if she had any hope he'd go away. "I'm in the bathroom," she yelled. "Leave me alone."

"You okay?"

She sighed. "Yes, I'm okay. Now go away."

She heard his laughter and rolled her eyes. Great, she thought. Now her paranoia is fodder for his comedy routine.

"Hey, you need to come get the phone. Mr. Jeffries wants to talk to you."

Kimberly groaned, not from stomach pains but the sharper pains of mental anguish. Mr. Jeffries must have found out. "All right, tell him I'll be there in a minute."

She didn't hear Bobby again so she assumed he'd gone downstairs. She opened the bathroom door and went into her room. She wished she could just cover herself up and disappear, but that wasn't going to happen. She pulled herself together and picked up the phone.

"Hello?"

"Kimberly, this is Mr. Jeffries."

"Yes —"

"Would you mind telling me what you thought you were doing when you promised the video would be ready for the Saturday night banquet?"

Kimberly closed her eyes and muttered a prayer for help and guidance to anyone within distance of hearing. "That's not what I meant —"

"How could you not mean to, Kimberly? I mean, he said you all but guaranteed it would be done."

A flash of anger flared deep inside her. She never said any such thing. Mr. Leonard had lied to Mr. Jeffries. "I didn't —"

She heard a sigh escape from Mr. Jeffries. "Never mind, Kimberly, I know how he is. It isn't all your fault. I do wish you had just left it to me."

She ground her toe into the carpet. "I'm sorry."

"We'll just have to get together and figure out how we can solve this."

"We can —" She stopped. It wasn't her project.

"We can what? Do you have any ideas?"

She knew the words wanted to squirm their way out of her mouth, but she refused to give in to the temptation. She couldn't jeopardize her relationship with Greg any more than she already had. "No, none."

"Fine," he said. "I'll call Greg and call a meeting for tomorrow after school."

Kimberly slammed the phone down with a thump, but no matter how loud a sound the phone made, the sound of her heart cracking was worse. The very thought of Jeffries talking to Greg filled her with dread.

Bobby bounded up the stairs and nearly ran into her. "Hey, Sis. What's up?"

"Nothing."

He stopped and turned back to her. "Why the long face?"

Kimberly wished he'd go away. "No reason, will you just leave me alone?"

From the look on his face, Kimberly thought she might have hurt her brother's feelings but then he opened his mouth.

"Leave me alone, leave me alone, leave me alone. I swear, Kimberly Anne, that's all I've ever heard out of you."

"So?" she said and slammed her bedroom door shut. What did he know about her problems? Nothing, that's what. Her life was blowing up in front of her face, and all Bobby did was bug her and bug her and bug her. "I thought you were leaving," she yelled.

Bobby instantly opened her door and looked in. "Not yet, sis. We have to transfer the title to the car."

Oh geez, she thought. Now make me really feel bad. Here he was, finally being a good guy and forking over his car and all she did was be her usual horrid self. She realized Bobby still held the door open. "I forgot," she muttered, "about the car, I mean."

Her brother stepped inside her room. "No problem, Sis."

That wasn't an invitation to come in, she thought, but instead said, "Yeah, it is. I shouldn't have mouthed off." She flopped over onto her stomach and pushed her face against a pillow as much to suggest Bobby might leave her room as to cover up her awkward and terrible feelings. The last thing she needed was her big brother playing "big brother."

But Bobby never could read her mind.

She heard her brother step into the room and come to the side of the bed.

"Hey, Kimbo," he said softly. "Can I help?"

She flung her arm out as if to push him away, but he kept on talking. "Look, maybe I can offer some advice. Or just be someone who will listen."

Kimberly rolled her head to one side and looked up. Her brother sounded like he cared. And she noticed that for the first time, she hadn't minded when he called her Kimbo.

"You want to help? You really will listen?"

He gave her one of those great bear-hug smiles of his and said, "Sure."

Then he dropped down onto the floor and faced her as she lay on her side in bed. She had pushed a pillow up against her stomach. "Are you hurt?" he asked and pointed to where the pillow covered her stomach.

She looked down. "No, I'm not hurt——at least not hurting that way."

Once again, her brother looked like he cared when she said that, and Kimberly felt an urge to tell him more. Instead, she asked, "Are you comfortable sitting on the floor like that?"

He looked down and shrugged. "Why?"

"Well, because you're so tall, and you look so uncomfortable."

"Hey, I thought we were going to talk about you."

Kimberly fought the sudden rush of tears pushing against her lids. "Okay," she said, finally giving in to the monumental pressure to confess her sins. "I made a really, really, really huge mistake today," she said and tried not to look at him full face but sort of glance at him sideways, as if that would make her confession any easier.

Bobby didn't say a word. Instead, he looked down at his folded hands. It's as if he understood her need to not meet his eyes directly.

"No one was in the video club room today after school. I was all alone when Mr. Leonard —"

"The principal?" he asked, interrupting.

"Yes, the principal," she answered before going on. "He wanted to speak to Mr. Jeffries or Greg —"

"Greg the boyfriend," he asked, still not looking at her.

"Yes," she sighed, "the boyfriend."

"Sorry."

"It's all right," she said. "The principal wanted us to have the video ready for Saturday night —"

"This Saturday —"

"Yes, Bobby, this Saturday," she said, trying hard not to let her growing frustration slip out. "I told him they weren't there but he insisted that I give him an answer." At this point, she felt a couple of tears slip out. "I didn't say we'd do it, I just said there might be a way. Then Mr. Leonard told Mr. Jeffries I guaranteed it would be ready for the banquet. That isn't what happened, Bobby, honest. I know I should have stayed out it and not even opened my mouth but——"

"You told Mr. Leonard he could have the video to show at the banquet."

Kimberly flinched when she heard him say what she did. "Not exactly," she said, her voice small and tight.

"Sounds like a real dilemma, Kimbo. What are you going to do?"

Kimberly flinched. "Me? Do? I'm not doing anything. Mr. Jeffries already called and bawled me out for even telling Mr. Leonard it might be possible———"

"Is it?"

Kimberly paused. She knew that would depend. It would depend on whether she or Greg were in control of the shoot. He had so much resistance to making changes at this late date, and he wouldn't want to shortchange the technical side. In her mind, she could see the storyboard, and she knew exactly what she'd do to make it happen.

She also saw what would happen if she even suggested the remedy. Greg would be furious with her for even suggesting what she wanted to do. The very thought of those light blue sky eyes turning dark and stormy cast a dark shadow over her soul. She'd rather stand outside and face the chance of lightning striking her dead than confess what she'd done and then tell him that, despite what he thought, she could pull it off.

No, that was not an option.

"No," she said, offering her brother no hope for a happy ending.

CHAPTER FIFTEEN

Her brother simply stared at her. He offered no solution and no resolution. If she had thought, he'd be of any help that thought was fading fast. Wasn't that just like him, she thought. Always appearing helpful but never totally putting himself out there. Disgusted, she turned her head to face the wall. What good can he offer?

She listened for signs of his leaving, but none came. She rose up on the bed and looked back at him. "You're still here?"

Bobby blinked, twice, before he answered. "Well, yeah, Kimbo. I said I'd listen."

She flopped down on the bed. "There's nothing left to tell."

She and her brother sat in the fading afternoon as the sun set and the outside matched the growing darkness in her soul. He hadn't said anything else since he said he'd listen, and she hadn't either. She was beginning to wonder if they weren't locked in some competition to see who could be quiet the longest. That would be just like Bobby——make everything a competition with her. She felt a flicker of anger as she listened to him breathe in and out, in and out, in and out.

"You know, you just don't get it," she finally said, her voice half-muffled by the pillow.

"Get what?"

"Anything, Bobby, you just don't get anything about me."

She heard him breathe in and out once, twice——

"I get you."

She waited to hear more but when it didn't come she turned over and stared at him. If she were only to see his shadow, she would have thought a big lumbering bear had come into her room and sat down next to her bed. "You don't get me," she said, her words spitting through her clenched teeth. "You don't get me; you have never gotten me, and you never will get me."

More silence. Then the sound of her brother's voice broke the silence and threatened to tear down all the walls she'd ever constructed to keep him at bay.

"Did I ever tell you what it was like the day you were born?" He didn't wait for her to answer. "Mom and Dad came home from the hospital, and they had you, all bundled in a green receiving blanket, and I had no idea what you would look like —I was barely seven then."

She heard her brother move and shift position, but she didn't stop his talking.

"You were adorable, Kimberly. And everyone loved you. Mom, Dad, Grandma and Grandpa, the neighbors, everyone. No one saw me anymore," he said, and she heard his voice falter. "I just disappeared from view."

She couldn't believe what he was saying. Her big larger-than-life brother who did everything and won everything once felt he didn't matter, didn't even exist——and all because she came into the world?

"The more I watched you take over Mom and Dad, the more I screamed for attention. Nothing worked until the day I came home with straight As. Mom and Dad made such a fuss over me, I loved it, absolutely loved it." Bobby sighed. "From that day forward, I vowed to excel at everything I tried. I'm still doing that."

Silence fell once more between them. Kimberly heard each of his words fall deep into her soul like nurturing pellets that opened and bloomed within. Her brother, her wonderful, exceptional brother had been jealous of her. She felt as though something struck the armor that had hardened around her heart and cracked it wide open. The casing fell apart, and Kimberly felt her true heart at last.

She looked at Bobby and saw him for the first time in her life. All the time she'd hardened her heart against him, wishing him ill, wanting him gone, envying his every thought, word and deed, only to discover that her brother had been jealous of her. She reached out and touched him on the shoulder. "I can't believe you were ever jealous of me. I'm sorry, Bobby. You do get me."

The two sat in the darkness for a while longer. Then she sat up, wiped the tears from her eyes, and patted him on the shoulder indicating he should get up, too. "I guess I need to figure out how I'm going to handle this mess I've created."

Bobby leaned down and gave her a sweet kiss on the cheek, then said, "You'll find a way, Sis. I know you will. But don't forget you have a big brother if you need him."

She smiled up at him. "I guess for starters, I could face the music with Mr. Jeffries."

The next day Kimberly got to school a half hour early. She wanted to catch Mr. Jeffries before homeroom. She found him in the visual arts room, of course, going over Greg's storyboard.

"What did Greg say?" she asked, hoping against all hope for the best.

"Well, you can imagine he's not happy."

She nodded.

"He doesn't think we can make Mr. Leonard's deadline. Even worse, he can't work on the project for the next several days."

If she'd had any doubts about the magnitude of her mistake, they were gone now. With Greg gone, there's no way they'd finish the video ahead of time. "Why can't he be here?"

"Family problems."

"Oh."

"He wants us to tell Principal Leonard that we can't make it by the banquet."

Kimberly digested his words slowly. "What will that mean?"

Mr. Jeffries gave a small laugh. "Well, he sure isn't going to be happy. Maybe, with Greg able to work on the project, we might have a chance but now...I just don't see it."

"I haven't seen Greg this morning. Will he be here for the afternoon meeting?"

"I doubt it. One of his brothers is in the hospital, and Greg has to help his mom out with the other kids. It sounded like he didn't expect to be back in school until Monday."

She knew he had to help his mom, but she had no idea he carried that much responsibility on his shoulders. Yes, she knew he had siblings and that he had to help his mom out a lot. Yes, she knew his dad had left them years ago, but she'd never appreciated the full magnitude of his responsibilities. If she examined her own life, she knew she'd come up short.

Kimberly felt worse than ever now that she knew she'd only added to Greg's increasing pressure and responsibilities. If she hadn't said so much to Mr. Leonard, he would never have expected them to deliver the video Saturday night. Maybe if she went to him....

The rest of the day slipped by, and Kimberly soon found herself standing outside the visual arts room. She wasn't sure she wanted to go inside. She had tried to talk to Mr. Leonard in the cafeteria during lunch but he dismissed her negative explanations and said he hardly thought the entire project could be held up due to one person, namely Greg Winters.

Fat lot he knew, she thought. Without Greg, the project could very well fall flat on its face. Kimberly hardly felt she had the needed technical skill to pull the entire project together and finish it one week ahead of schedule.

But what was she to do? Mr. Jeffries had said Greg wouldn't be back until Monday. Ricardo had even confirmed Greg's absence and said he didn't see any way that Greg would be able to devote even one night to the project. Kimberly had screwed things up royally.

At first she didn't want to know what Greg thought about her and her meddling, but finally she sat next to Ricardo in the cafeteria and asked him.

"Chica, what to you expect? He is not a happy man."

Kimberly sat and waited.

"What do you want me to say, amiga? That all will be well, and you and Greg will live happily ever after?" He glanced over at her, and then offered her half of his sandwich. "Can't do it. Wish I could."

Kimberly wished he could, too. Oh, how she wished it but she knew it was a useless wish because it would never happen. She left Ricardo with his sandwich and his thoughts and sat down at a table by herself. Somehow she would have to come to the rescue and make it all work—but how?

How? Seemed like "how" was a recurring theme for Kimberly. By the end of the day, she still had not figured out how she could bring the project to a complete finish. She also had not seen Greg and had begun to realize that she might not get to talk to him until next week. That was way too long. She couldn't let his anger at her fester over the weekend. She'd have no hope of forgiveness if she did that.

And what about the malicious gossip Carol had been spreading. It was bad enough before all this mess with the principal, but now Carol's fury had gone into high gear and Kimberly had learned Carol blamed her for just about everything possible. Kimberly this, Kimberly that. Guess what Kimberly did now. Rumors all of them, but they still hurt. She'd tried talking to Carol, but the girl just walked off, leaving Kimberly standing in the middle of the hall with her mouth open, still talking. She'd tried Ricardo, but he simply threw up his hands and said he didn't know what to do about Carol. He was tired of her constant jealousy, always accusing him of having a thing for Marla, always berating him for every moment he wasn't with her. Kimberly had even gone to Marla for help. At least she'd tried to comfort Kimberly but in the end she said she was sorry, but Greg wasn't even listening to her anymore. When it came to the video project, Greg had told Marla he couldn't believe Kimberly had actually gone over his head and promised the principal he'd get a finished video by the night of the banquet.

At the end of the day, Kimberly was desolate. She'd lost Greg, lost her best friend, probably put her internship on the video project in jeopardy and highly annoyed Mr. Jeffries. She didn't see how things could get much worse.

Now she was expected to face even more music by going in and facing the video club members and explaining herself. Mr. Jeffries drove a hard bargain when he told her the only way she could salvage her position with the project was to attend the meeting and tell the members why she did what she did. He also said it wouldn't hurt if she had an answer or two when they asked her how they were going to meet the new deadline.

She thought it would be a good idea, too. Unfortunately, she didn't have any ideas to offer the club. Short of a miracle, Kimberly hadn't a clue as to how they were going to satisfy Mr. Leonard's demand for the video Saturday night. Kimberly sank down onto one of the benches that lined the hallway near the visual arts building. She watched several of the students working on the video walk toward the classroom. She had no idea how she'd get through the next hour, let alone the next few days.

She thought of Greg, the one person who had brought her so much happiness over the last few weeks. He had been there through the rows with Carol, through the misunderstandings with Marla, even through her fits and fights with her brother. Now, at a time when she needed him most, he was gone. More than gone, Kimberly feared Greg had made a decision about her that would cause him to leave her life forever.

That was a fate too dark to think about, so Kimberly left the bench and headed for the door to the visual arts room. She only hoped the video club didn't skin her alive for her rash promise.

CHAPTER SIXTEEN

No one said a word when she entered the classroom. Kimberly had no idea they could be that quiet. Mr. Jeffries waved her forward, and she stood at the front of the room. She felt their stares, their silent accusations. She had a feeling that if they thought they could, they'd put her in the stocks for a day or two. Kimberly was thankful she lived in the 21st century.

"I guess you've all heard," she began and the answering voices swelled in response. "I know it was a mistake. I should have just stayed out of it, but it's done. I'm sorry."

She went on to explain in detail how Mr. Leonard had come into the room and how he told her what he wanted and what he expected her to deliver. After she had finished, she stood at the front and waited. She expected them to hurl taunts or cry out questions but instead they all sat and stared at her. She had prepared for their insults, not their silence. She looked at Mr. Jeffries but he didn't respond. So he was giving her the silent treatment, too?

She wondered how long she would have to stand there before someone took pity on her.

Finally, she heard Marla speak. "Kimberly has apologized. She's told us how it happened. She explained how Mr. Leonard ambushed her the other day. I think we all should stop a minute and think about what our reaction would have been. I'm not sure I would have done anything different."

Kimberly didn't know what to say. She hadn't expected Marla to be the first to come to her defense. She glanced down the rows of faces and wondered what each one was thinking. Were they receptive at all to Marla's speech?

Mr. Jeffries then spoke. "Marla is right. We need to refocus and think about how we can make this happen."

Kimberly heard some noise at the back of the room, a bit of loud whispering among several of the girls. She realized with a sinking heart that the sounds came from the area around Carol.

Carol stood up. "I don't think Kimberly should get off this easy. She had no right to speak for us, for Greg, for you, Mr. Jeffries. Marla's just trying to defend her new friend."

Marla stood ready to counter Carol's words, but Ricardo spoke first. "I agree with Marla."

"What," Carol said, anger tingeing the edges of her voice. "You're sticking up for Kimberly and agreeing with Marla? That's rich."

"That's enough," Mr. Jeffries said, his voice making it clear that the debate had ended. "Everyone come down here and take a look at the storyboard and see what we have left to do. We need to have a real brainstorming session if we're to have any hope of getting this project finished by the weekend."

All the kids gathered in front of Greg's storyboard, all except Carol. Kimberly started toward her, but Carol stomped angrily out of the room. Her departure left a hole in Kimberly's heart. She wondered if they'd ever be friends again.

They poured over the storyboard and script for the next hour. Mr. Jeffries had them group into threes and fours, each charged with finding a solution. He and Kimberly remained at the front of the room discussing alternatives. Finally, Kimberly felt like the makings of a real possibility taking shape. She would have to condense several scenes, change up a couple of locations, and get the remaining video shot tomorrow, but the plan would work. She could begin the editing tonight. Mr. Jeffries agreed to keep the visual arts room open late.

Ricardo, Marla, and Kimberly worked feverishly for hours and then sat huddled in front of the computer as Kimberly worked the editing software. They were so engrossed in the process that they didn't hear the lab door open.

"Hey, what's up," Greg said as he approached them.

For a split second, Kimberly thought he'd forgiven her, but then she realized he simply hadn't seen her. Marla and Ricardo blocked his view. When Greg did make eye contact with her, a frown replaced his smile. He stared at the computer screen.

"Are you editing?" Greg asked as he pushed through Ricardo and Marla. "That's the first day's shoot."

Kimberly didn't know whether she should act surprised, happy or just plain scared. She had no idea what he was going to say or do. They hadn't spoken since Mr. Jeffries tipped him off about the banquet deadline.

She raised her right hand, slightly, in a greeting, but Greg didn't respond.

"Why are you working on the video?"

"Take a look," Ricardo said. "Mr. J came up with a few suggestions, and that got us started. Kimberly's managed to

come up with some more ways we can pare down the video."
Ricardo pointed to the storyboard. "Take a look."

Kimberly flinched and kept editing. She didn't want to face
Greg. Marla patted Kimberly on the shoulder as if that would
somehow help Kimberly's resolve. Kimberly waited for Greg's
reaction.

Greg studied the changes. After a while, he shook his head and
turned back to the trio still waiting at the computer. "You can't
be serious," he said, clenching and unclenching his hands.

Kimberly had reviewed the changes a number of times and each
time she came away fully confident in the revision. "I don't
understand," she replied. "We've attacked this from every angle
and the results have been same. It'll work."

Greg turned back to the pages on the board. "I don't see it. If
you change up this scene, it will have an effect on all the future
scenes."

Kimberly got up from the computer and stood next to Greg.
"No, no, it won't. If you read further, you'll see that we're
collapsing several scenes." She pointed to several red crosses
showing entire passages deleted. "I know we can do this."

Greg faced Ricardo and Marla. "Are you onboard with this?"

Marla said yes right away, but Ricardo took a few minutes.
Kimberly felt for him. Having differing opinions and
contrasting solutions can make or break a friendship. She could
see the surprise on Greg's face. He had expected Ricardo to
back him, no questions asked.

Finally, Ricardo shook his head as if he was throwing off cobwebs, and went to the storyboard and pointed. "If we do all this we can probably eliminate a day or two of editing. If we do that —"

Greg put his hand up to stop Ricardo. "Would you give us a few minutes — alone?"

"Of course," Marla replied, although Kimberly did notice that she had a quizzical look. "We'll wait in the hall."

The computer screen turned black, returning to hibernation mode, and Kimberly thought the machine had the better deal. For the first time, she did not want to be with Greg.

He waited until the classroom door closed before he launched his attack. "When did you become head of the video project? You're not even a member of the senior team. You're an intern, just an intern. Get it?"

Greg's anger continued to fuel his assault. "I don't have time for all this," he said, waving toward the red-lined storyboard.

Kimberly rushed on, hoping Greg would eventually discover the light in her solution. "We don't need you. We can do this ourselves. We have it all worked out."

She regretted the words as soon as they left her mouth, but it was too late. Her sharp words hit him hard. Although she couldn't see his eyes, his stooped shoulders said volumes.

If this was winning, she didn't want any part of it.

CHAPTER SEVENTEEN

Kimberly stood in the visual arts classroom and felt utterly alone. The whiteboard teased her with the scribbled results from the groups mass brainstorming session. The storyboard held the red-inked changes made to Greg's vision. Someone had pulled the blinds and blocked the bright afternoon sun. After all the hype and excitement of the earlier hours when she, Ricardo, and Marla had sought ways to make the new vision work, she had about as much energy as a movie script's worked-to-death saggy middle.

Greg had gone, and with his exit he robbed her of her creativity, her excitement, and her confidence. She plopped down on the chair at the computer and stared at the black screen. Too bad she didn't have a cave to crawl into and die.

From the look of things, her first-blush romance had died, too.

The door opened, and Ricardo and Marla rushed to her aid.

"What happened?" Marla asked. "Greg didn't bother to say good-bye to either one of us."

Ricardo bent down on one knee and rubbed her empty palm. "What's the matter? Your fingers are icy cold."

Not as cold as Greg's heart, she thought.

* * *

That night, Kimberly tossed and turned, rolled and spun in her bed. No matter what, she couldn't get comfortable. She knew her idea would work. Why couldn't Greg see it? She listened for a sound, any sound, from her laptop that would signal a friend on the other end of the Internet highway. But there were no rings or alarms alerting her to an email or an instant message.

Greg Winters had cast a long shadow over her heart and her aspirations. He wanted to work slowly and steadily, like a good workhorse. Not Kimberly. She sped forward throwing ideas here and there, turning everything into a competition. Even her fledgling romance had turned into a churning mess.

She flopped over, punched her pillowcase and used it as a neck rest. Tomorrow she had to guide the video team toward making the right cuts and working out the many details that would make her job in the editing room much easier. It would be so much easier if Greg had tried to help out.

He didn't.

She understood. His responsibilities far outweighed her own. She didn't have any lives depending on her in the arena where her dreams and goals often collided with each other. At best, she was only responsible for herself. It didn't help that she had stupidly and cruelly told him he wasn't needed.

Finally, Kimberly felt the first tugs of a deep sleep calling her, so she closed her eyes and hoped she'd wake to a new day full of promise and possibilities.

* * *

The next morning, the morning of the banquet, in a flurry of agitation and excitement, Kimberly found herself behind the camera, directing the actors. They had done as much as they could over the last few afternoons and evenings, but she finally had to admit another trip to the Henderson Building was in order. She stood on top of the roof and exhaled, trying to steady her nerves. Ricardo stood nearby. She wondered if he remained close as a show of support or in case of an emergency.

She had decided to block the scenes on the run, and everything seemed to be going well. Marla had no trouble with her lines, Carol had managed to get everyone into an early call for make-up, and Ricardo and the others made it to the location early.

She had returned to the Henderson Building to re-shoot and compress a number of scenes. Everywhere she went she was met with reminders of that first shoot with Greg. That blistering image of him sweating and rolling an iced water bottle across his forehead vied with the memory of their close talk under the shade of the scrim on the roof. Like a cobweb, her memories had been stranded together and at the moment she stirred one memory, all others would thrum in concert.

She had hoped Greg would have a free moment and stop by but she wasn't surprised when he didn't. After the morning shoot, she and Mr. Jeffries had agreed to meet in the visual arts classroom to go review the final edit. She could afford to worry about the editing later. First, she had to get good video.

* * *

She drove into the near empty parking lot at Northrupp High thirty minutes late. She rushed out of the car, grabbed the equipment she would need right away and half-ran, half-skipped to the steel doors that opened into the building that led to the visual arts classroom and where, she hoped, Mr. Jeffries waited.

Her footsteps echoed through the empty building as she sped down the corridor. Naturally the classroom had to be at the end of the hall. Mr. Jeffries must have left the door open because she saw light spilling onto the hallway tile. She slowed down as she got closer to the room. Even though she was late, Mr. J might not appreciate her running down the hall while she carried the equipment, especially the new camera.

"Ricardo called and told me you were on your way," he said as he shifted papers on his desk.

"Sorry to keep you waiting. We found the perfect angle for a great shot in the stairwell and decided to go for it."

"Do you know what you're going to do?"

"Yes, I have most of it blocked out, and Ricardo's going to join me in an hour."

"Good," he said and stood, ready to go. "The editing program is up and running. Listen, I have an errand to run, but I'll be back in a few hours. Will you— "

"Don't worry. Everything's under control."

Later, Kimberly would wonder why she ever thought she could do it all by herself.

CHAPTER EIGHTEEN

K imberly picked up where she, Ricardo and Marla had left off the night before. They had managed to condense and edit a rather tight segment on the roof, and she hoped today's work would help streamline the video even more. As she worked, she lost herself in the process. Her intense concentration held her captive and oblivious to the real world.

The sound of her name blasted her back into the visual arts classroom. She turned around and saw Carol at the doorway. She had her guitar with her.

"Hey," Kimberly said, waving her into the room. She wasn't that happy to see Carol. As much as she'd loved Carol in the past, right now her former best friend spelled T-R-O-U-B-L-E. Kimberly didn't need any more problems if she planned on getting the video ready for the banquet later that evening.

"I saw your car and thought I'd say hello."

Well, that's a lie, Kimberly thought, knowing Carol knew Kimberly had to be here to finish the edit. If she wants to pretend, it's an accidental meeting, whatever. A blast of thunder punctuated Kimberly's last thought.

"Started to rain," Carol said, pulling a chair nearer to the computer and Kimberly. Her hair gleamed with the wide streak of emerald green. "You're busy. I know. I—"

Kimberly stopped what she was doing and faced her friend, the former friend. She tried not to show her exasperation but Carol made it difficult. "What?"

"I want to tell you I'm sorry."

"That's nice." Kimberly returned to the computer and tapped a string of keys. Why didn't Carol understand that this was not a good time for a re-bonding session? "Sorry, I have to get this done."

"I,—Kimberly, I want us to go back to being friends." Carol seemed to shrink in size as soon as the words escaped. She played with her silver thumb ring. "I miss you. I miss us."

Kimberly listened.

Carol shifted in her seat, then rose and walked over to the industrial shelf that housed every type of media the club had found: vinyl records, 8-tracks, turntables, reel-to-reels, CDs and now DVDs. "I'm sorry, truly sorry. I should never have talked against you. Ricardo was right. I was such a fool."

Kimberly couldn't believe her friend of ten-plus years came out and admitted to spreading the rumors. She had expected Carol to ignore and deny any part in them. Kimberly swiveled her chair to get a better look at Carol, but all she saw was her back. Kimberly didn't want to think about all this. She tried to squelch the sick feeling of betrayal that spread through her mind and increased her level of anxiety.

"I was jealous. I'm sorry. You know how I get about Ricardo. I was so upset with Marla talking to Ricardo, and then you seemed to stick up for my number one enemy and left me stranded on the outside. It hurt. "

"Hey, we all make mistakes," Kimberly said, acutely aware of her recent failings. Was she any better than Carol? Kimberly liked to think she'd treat her friends better, but she understood all too well how things could quickly get out of hand.

Carol tried to smile, but Kimberly saw the pain in her eyes as she spoke. "I thought I was losing you. You've been my best friend for so long. I didn't want to share you. I'm so sorry."

Kimberly felt the same pain. She'd missed Carol, missed her company. "Why don't we try to put all this in the past. Let's not think or talk about it anymore for now."

Carol, whose chain link belt with hot silver medallions jangled as she walked, came toward Kimberly with outstretched arms. "I'd call for a group hug but it's just you and me," Carol said in between Kimberly's sudden laughter and weepy tears of joy.

"What about Ricardo? You've been pretty mean to him the last week or so."

"I know. We already talked about it," Carol said. "He's wonderful and I'm such a fool."

Kimberly hugged Carol. She was glad they'd come to an agreement and were friends again. She didn't know if they'd ever be able to be as close as they were before all this mess, but at least they had a new beginning. New beginnings brought new hope. Then she thought of one new test for Carol. 'Marla will be stopping by anytime, now. Are you good with that?"

Carol nodded and continued to wipe her face. "I'm good. I'm definitely good. I know I've been a fool. I've promised Ricardo and now you to change. I've been jealous of Marla; I've envied you. It nearly cost me everyone I cared about. I want to change. I promise, I will. "

* * *

When Carol left, Kimberly returned to her work. Things had been going so well she thought she'd have time to spare to finish the project. She brought up the new footage and looked. She looked at some more. She'd made a huge mistake.

"Hey, how's it going?"

"Time Code."

"What's wrong?" Ricardo glanced at the computer screen then back to Kimberly's wet face. "I thought you said everything was moving ahead of schedule?"

Kimberly couldn't stop the tell-tale tears.

"What about it?"

"Look, I messed up the time code."

"Stop with the tears," he said and patted her back. "We'll fix it. I don't know how we'll get it all done on time, but we will."

Ricardo's reaction was measured and way less than Kimberly had expected. As if she hadn't already invited disaster, it now seemed that the video gods had joined together to thwart her at every turn to make it impossible for her to have the video ready for Mr. Leonard later that night. She should have left everything alone. She should have never rushed things. Her massive mess had now turned into a disaster. Sure, they can get it done, but it will take hours to fix the time code problem. She knew she'd skewed the entire editing process and within hours of the deadline. She would never be able to finish and meet Mr. Leonard's demands.

"Don't worry," Ricardo said and reached behind and pulled out his phone. He speed-dialed a number and did some very fast talking.

Kimberly's crying had been reduced to a ragged burst of sniffles when her worst fears materialized. Mr. Leonard entered the visual arts room.

"Kimberly, how's the video coming? We've got a full house tonight, and I'm counting on you." Mr. Leonard had wandered over to where Ricardo sat at the computer. "Are you two almost finished?"

Kimberly opened her mouth to confess and beg forgiveness, but Ricardo managed to get his answer in first.

"You'll have it, sir. It may be close to viewing time, but we'll deliver." Ricardo never took his eyes and fingers off the computer.

Kimberly stared open-mouthed at Ricardo. She couldn't imagine how he thought they'd be able to fix the new problems and still keep Mr. Leonard happy. When the principal turned away from Ricardo, he leaned back in his chair and mouthed the words: don't worry.

Mr. Leonard seemed happy enough with Ricardo's answer because he quickly left the building.

"What were you thinking?" she said, her voice sounding harsh and shrill even to her own ears. She rolled her chair back to the computer. "I don't understand."

Ricardo smiled and patted her on the back. "You will, my friend. You will.

CHAPTER NINETEEN

Kimberly had lost hope, but Ricardo pushed her to continue. The minutes turned into half-hours, and the half-hours turned into hours. Ricardo set to work to fix the time code problem but it was slow, tedious work, and Kimberly worried that he would never get it all done. More than once she had to fight to keep back the tears. She'd been so foolish and all she did was make things worse. She never seemed to solve problems. Her gift apparently lay in creating them.

She was hard at work when she heard footsteps behind her. She turned quickly.

"Greg, what are you doing here?" He's like magic, she thought. He appears out of nowhere.

Greg immediately moved behind Ricardo, so he could watch what Ricardo was doing on the computer. "Problems?"

Ricardo nodded. "A few."

She was acutely aware of Greg's presence. "How are you? I thought you wouldn't be able to help us out this weekend."

He shoved his hands in his back pockets and wandered around the tables and desks that played host the various equipment. "Things changed. They released my brother from the hospital, and he's home with my mom. Everything is fine."

She stopped what she was doing. "If you're free, you should be in control of what we're doing. Ricardo, show Greg what we tried."

Greg bent over Ricardo and stared at the screen. A couple of times he nodded as if in agreement with something, other times he seemed surprised. Finally, he grabbed a chair so he could sit side-to-side with Ricardo. In minutes he'd taken control of the software and was working away.

Ricardo leaned back to give him room and grinned at Kimberly.

At one point, Greg raised his head and smiled at the two of them. "This is good, guys. Really good."

Kimberly felt like a sunburst had exploded inside her body and an incredible warm and cozy feeling spread like a river through her veins, relaxing her muscles and easing the tension she'd carried for days. She leaned back in her chair and watched Greg work the keyboard. She picked up her cell phone and called her brother. She wanted to be sure he'd still be home when her work on the video had finished. Bobby had been so open and honest with her during their heart-to-heart talk. She wanted to spend more time with him.

Mr. Leonard stopped by on his way to the banquet. He seemed impressed with the work everyone was doing and attempted to kid around with them. Greg promised he would deliver the video himself as soon as they'd finished.

Finally, the finishing touches were applied, and the new senior video project was marked "done." Greg turned off the computer; Ricardo began re-shelving the equipment and material that they'd used earlier that morning. Kimberly rose to stop him.

"Hey, that's my job. I'm the intern, you know," she said and started for the table where she'd put most of the equipment that had been used at the Henderson Building.

Ricardo put his hand out as if he were protecting the equipment and trying to keep her away. "No way," he said and nodded toward Greg. "You need to take care of more important things."

"Sure?"

"Positive. Now go."

Greg had shut down the computer and was cleaning up the area around the workstation. Kimberly came up beside him. "I wanted to thank you for coming tonight. We would have never been able to pull it off without you."

He shook his head, and then he turned and reached over, putting his hands on her shoulders and staring directly into her eyes. "I am so sorry. I have been such a fool."

"You? No, me. Look at the way I treated Marla. I envied her relationship with you. Now she's turned out to be a great friend."

"I had a lot of time to think when I was home with the kids. Things were touch and go with my brother for a day or two when he was in the hospital. The doctors were worried because his fever was so high for so long." Greg's voice grew soft as he talked about his brother. "I realized how much I care about the people in my life—and that includes you."

She started to say something, but he put his fingers to her lips. "There's more," he said. "The other day I knew you had come up with a viable way to get the video ready for tonight. I just didn't want it to be you who came up with the ideas. I'm an overbearing, critical jerk who felt threatened by your obvious natural talent and your dedication to the craft."

She felt the weight of his hands on her shoulders. They felt comfortable, as though they belonged there. A series of emotions rolled through her. Finally, she gained some control and spoke. "I think we're both a little guilty. I was way too quick to try to prove you wrong, or worse, to even best you at your own game." She shook her head thinking about her relationship with her brother. "I'm way too competitive. I should never have assumed your role."

Greg shushed her. "Forget the past. It's over. If there's one thing I've learned from you, it's that there is so much more to life than I ever imagined."

She stroked his hands, still resting comfortably on her shoulders. "I'm too much in a hurry. I need to slow down, to take the time to learn the technical side. I need to learn to cooperate instead of compete."

When he pulled her down into a chair and sat next to her, she welcomed the memories of a creaking swing, a poolside party, and a noisy bird named Amos. When he pulled her close, all her insecurities slipped away. When she closed her eyes, she could see them crossing the finish line together.

And when they kissed, she finally understood that to win love you had to give love.

DISCUSSION GROUP QUESTIONS

In VIDEO MAGIC, Kimberly confronts the many faces of jealousy as she struggles to balance friends, family, and school. In one survey, 30% of teens said they had to deal with some form of jealousy. Feeling a little envious might be okay, but usually the green-eyed monster comes between friends, creates tension in families, and tears apart teen romantic relationships.

1. How do the different characters in VIDEO MAGIC express jealousy? Can you identify the different forms in which jealousy appears in the story?
2. What did the characters do that made you think they were jealous? Do you think they were right in their feelings?
3. In the story Kimberly is upset when her brother comes home for a visit. Why?
4. Are there any "favorites" in your family? Why do you think that family member is the "favorite?"
5. What other feelings can also be associated with jealousy? Anger? Suspicion? What else?
6. Have you ever lost a friend due to your jealous feelings?
7. Do you know what it means to "covet" something? Were you ever jealous of something someone owned? Have you ever been envious?
8. Is there ever a time when it's okay to be a little bit jealous? Can you find an example in the story when jealous feelings led to something positive?
9. Have you ever felt jealous when a friend has started dating??
10. What else can trigger a jealous reaction between friends, family members, or dating partners?
11. Is jealousy a sign of love? Explain.
12. What can someone do to tame their "the jealous monster?"

Vikk Simmons

ABOUT THE AUTHOR

Vikk Simmons is a full-time writer and author of the *In Love at Northrupp High* teen romance series. Do you enjoy old-fashioned, classic romance stories? Vikk does. She loves to write about young love, especially that window from those early moments when the girl and the boy first meet to that special moment when they realize they are in love. From the beginning, love is a delicate dance. The rhythm changes, the steps become more complicated, and the two have some learning to do if they want to perfect the dance.

Life is messy and complicated. Vikk knows that all too well. She lives in Houston, Texas and shares her life with six dogs and two cats. A confirmed bibliophile, she enjoys reading as much as writing, but you'll also find her outside walking the dogs, gardening, and sharing life over a cup of coffee with a friend at the local bookstore.

Visit Vikk's Amazon Author Page:

amazon.com/author/vikksimmons

Vikk Simmons

About the In Love at Northrupp High series

Northrup High is the fictional setting for the *In Love at Northrupp High* teen romance series. The high school is in Houston, Texas, and the stories revolve around the characters who attend Northrupp High.

While each story features a new couple, don't be surprised if you see some of your favorite characters reappearing in the series. The characters are totally fictional, but the author does admit that bits and pieces of people she's known often show up in her books with a little bit of this one and a little bit of that all mixed together to create somebody new.

Look for these titles:

VIDEO MAGIC

DIVIDED LOYALTIES

DRAMA DIVAS

ABOUT DIVIDED LOYALTIES

Before John Higheagle came into her life, sixteen year old Trisha Braedon thought she had it all under control: school, her college scholarship, and her parents divorce. But the gentle, charming newcomer, with his environmental causes and crusading spirit, isn't like anyone Trisha had ever known. Their instant attraction to each other draws Trisha into Jon's world of passionate involvement in environmental causes. But her participation puts her much needed scholarship at risk and creates even more conflict in her already troubled family life. Feeling torn and divided on every front, Trisha finds her loyalty questioned everywhere she goes. Finally, the unresolved issues are forced into the open and Trisha must deal with the truth about her feelings, her family and her relationship with Jon.

ℬℭℬℭℬℭℬℭℬℭℬℭ

Be the first to know when *DIVIDED LOYALTIES* and *DRAMA DIVAS*, the next two books in the *In Love at Northrupp High* series, are released and get advance notice of special promotions. You won't want to miss them. Also, receive email updates and news. Go to:

NorthruppHighNews.com

SNEAK PEAK OF DIVIDED LOYALTIES

Trisha fell behind as she stopped to examine a row of Hopi Kachinas. One in particular caught her attention, and she played her fingers down the deeply carved shape, tracing the design of a bundle of corn etched into a squared mask. Her hand moved to another, a painted black and red clown, then another. She admired the detail and wondered how long someone had spent carving these ancient gods. As her attention left the Kachinas, she heard the sound of the flute again. Turning slightly, she followed the sound of flute notes to a stall where an older man, dressed in buckskin pants and shirt, beaded moccasins and wearing a single black threaded dream catcher in his ear, sat on a wooden stool and played a wooden flute. Trisha stood off to the side and pretended to search among the discs of Native American music, all the while listening, captivated by the sweet melodies. A line of wooden flutes lay on the table in front of her.

"Ever played?"

Startled, Trisha turned and found Jon holding a flute. She'd been so mesmerized by the music she hadn't even noticed him pulling one of the flutes from the table. "No, not at all. You?"

"Some, when I lived on the reservation I used to go off into one canyon in particular and practice." That said, Jon lifted the flute to his lips and trilled out a couple of notes.

The flute player stopped his own playing and smiled. "It would seem at least one of you is familiar with the flute. You know Carlos Nakai, then?" he asked Jon.

"Some," he said again.

"And you," the flute player said to Trisha. "You're aware of the custom of the flute playing?"

Trisha looked at both of them, then shook her head and smiled. "No, but the music is beautiful."

"Long ago the flutes were used as a courting instrument. Young men would sit outside the tipi of their loved one and play one love song after another in an attempt to win her heart." The old man tipped his flute toward Jon. "You are looking for a good flute, perhaps? One that sings from the heart?"

Jon accepted the flute the old man gave him and put it to his lips. Fingering the flute, he played a delicate and pure melody that wrapped itself around the chambers of Trisha's heart and she felt herself stop breathing. The sweltering heat of the tent only intensified the moment. The smell of burning sage tickled her nose, the parade of people pressed past, the ringing of conch bells ran counterpoint with the flute. Trisha had never heard anything so beautiful as the song Jon played on the old man's flute. When he had finished he offered the flute back to the old man, but, with tears in his eyes, the man refused, saying, "No, no, she's yours. She's never played so sweetly for me. You must take her and name her and she will be yours forever."

Jon nodded, his dark eyes shining. "Thank you," he said, his voice soft as the prairie wind blowing over the fields. "I will listen for the name and treat her with the honor she deserves." With that, he placed the flute inside a leather pouch at his side.

The old man smiled and nodded gently toward Trisha. "You have a captive audience already."

Jon waited a beat, then smiled and spoke quietly. "One I fully intend to use."

Don't forget! Sign up to receive news, updates, and special promotions for *DIVIDED LOYALTIES* and all the books in the *In Love at Northrupp High* series. Go sign up now!

NorthruppHighNews.com